MOLLY MALONE & BRAM STOKER IN

THE RIDDLE OF THE DISAPPEARING DICKENS

'An absolute riot of a read – funny and page-turning
with some of the most eye-watering puns in history.'
Louie Stowell, author of the Loki *series*

'Molly and Bram are the barmiest, best and most
brilliant duo around. There's no mystery why kids
love these books so much.'
Shane Hegarty, author of the Darkmouth *series*

'Alan Nolan is at the top of his game as he guides
you through the cobble-stoned, foggy alleyways
of Victorian London, hot on the tail of a mystery
worthy of Sherlock Holmes himself!'
Gary Northfield, author of the Julius Zebra *series*

ALAN NOLAN grew up in Windy Arbour, Dublin and now lives in Bray, Co. Wicklow with his wife and three children. This is Alan's third book about Molly Malone and Bram Stoker; their first two adventures are *The Sackville Street Caper* and *Double Trouble at the Dead Zoo*. Alan is the author and illustrator of *Fintan's Fifteen*, *Conor's Caveman* and the *Sam Hannigan* series, and is the illustrator of *Animal Crackers: Fantastic Facts About Your Favourite Animals*, written by Sarah Webb. He runs illustration and writing workshops for children, and you may see him lugging his drawing board and pencils around your school or local library.

www.alannolan.ie

X: @alnolan

Instagram: @alannolan_author

MOLLY MALONE & BRAM STOKER IN

THE RIDDLE OF THE DISAPPEARING DICKENS

ALAN NOLAN

THE O'BRIEN PRESS
DUBLIN

First published 2024 by
The O'Brien Press Ltd,
12 Terenure Road East, Rathgar,
Dublin 6, D06 HD27, Ireland.
Tel: +353 1 4923333; Fax: +353 1 4922777
E-mail: books@obrien.ie
Website: obrien.ie

The O'Brien Press is a member of Publishing Ireland
ISBN: 978-1-78849-502-8

Layout and design by Emma Byrne
Cover illustration by Shane Cluskey
Internal illustration p 234 by Shane Cluskey
Map, posters and internal chapter header illustrations by Alan Nolan
Author photograph p 2 by Sam Nolan

8 7 6 5 4 3 2 1
28 27 26 25 24

Printed and bound by Nørhaven Paperback A/S, Denmark.

The paper in this book is produced using pulp from managed forests

Published in
DUBLIN
UNESCO
City of Literature

Growing up with
O'BRIEN
obrien.ie

MIX
Paper | Supporting
responsible forestry
FSC® C104608

DEDICATION

For Isla

TABLE OF CONTENTS

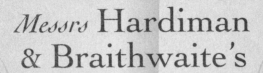

Messrs Hardiman & Braithwaite's

Patented Map *of* Dublin City
1858
Updated Edition 1859

BRUNSWICK STREET

UPPER C

KING STREET

KING STREET

GT BRITAIN ST

MINICK ST

KING STREET

Debtors' Prison

HENRY STREET

Smithfield Market

LITTLE MARY STREET

St Michan's Church

CAPEL ST

KING'S INN QUAY

RIVER LIFFEY

RIVER LIFFEY

BRIDGE ST

COOK ST

Dublin Castle

HIGH STREET

CASTLE ST

THOMAS ST

FRANCIS STREET

PATRICK STREET

BRIDE STREET

To Clontarf & Howth

Billy the Pan's Family Home

BUCKINGHAM STREET

GARDINER STREET

GLOUCESTER STREET

Bram's House

PALACE ROW

FREDERICK ST

GRANBY ROW

The Rotunda Round Room

SACKVILLE STREET

MARLBOROUGH STREET

MABBOT STREET

GT BRITAIN ST

Nelson's Pillar

COLES LANE

HENRY STREET

General Post Office

NORTH WALL

ABBEY STREET

EDEN QUAY

RIVER LIFFEY

GEORGE'S QUAY

CARLISLE BRIDGE

Ha'penny Bridge

TEMPLE BAR

TOWNSEND STREET

COLLEGE GREEN

GT BRUNSWICK STREET

DAME STREET

ALLEYWAY

Trinity College

GREAT GEORGE ST

EXCHEQUER STREET

GRAFTON STREET

NASSAU STREET

DAWSON ST

KILDARE ST

To Kingstown

A Short List of Characters Contained Within, Provided by the Most Considerate Author for Your Instruction and Delight:

BRAM STOKER
The future author of *Dracula*, almost twelve years of age, yearns for adventure and to have stories to tell.

MOLLY MALONE
Twelve years of age, accomplished sneak thief and part-time fishmonger.

SHEP, ROSE, BILLY THE PAN, HETTY HARDWICKE, CALICO TOM, AKA THE SACKVILLE STREET SPOOKS
Molly's gang of child pickpockets, to whom she is part sergeant major, part mother hen.

CHARLES DICKENS
World-renowned author of wonderful books such as *A Christmas Carol*, *Oliver Twist*, *Little Dorrit*, *The Old Curiosity Shop*, etc., etc., etc.

HENRY 'HARRY' DICKENS
Charles' eleven-year-old son, an aspiring magician, and his father's greatest fan.

MADAME FLORENCE FLORENCE
A fortune teller, variously known as the Seer of the What-Is-To-Come, the One Who Knows All, the Seventh Daughter of a Seventh Daughter, and the White Witch of Westmoreland Street.

MR BERTRAM 'WILD BERT' FLORENCE
A semi-retired Wild West trick-rider, zebra-wrangler and pony-vaulter, and Madame Flo's husband.

LADY H
A mysterious, aristocratic woman who dresses completely in black.

MR GRIMBLE AND MR BLEAT
Lady H's two thuggish cockney henchmen, both born within hearing of the Bow Bells.

BOUNDERBY AND CADDSWORTH
A pair of bumbling detectives, one with a moustache and no beard, the other with a beard and no moustache.

MR ABRAHAM STOKER & MRS CHARLOTTE STOKER
Bram's father and mother – his father is a strait-laced civil servant and Keeper of the Crown Jewels at Dublin Castle; his mother is a skilled storyteller and incurable chatterbox.

AND, FOR AN ENCORE ...

The renowned author bowed low, the bobble on his long nightcap sweeping across the polished wooden boards of the stage as he allowed the rapturous applause of the adoring audience to wash over him. The red curtains swished closed, ruffling the soft, greying hair that stood out comically from either side of the cap, and the great man, drained from yet another dramatic reading from his most famous book, slumped into the chair beside his reading table.

He pulled the blue–and–white striped cap from his head, slung it onto the velvet-topped lectern beside the battered copy of *A Christmas Carol* that he always brought along but seldom referred to, and sighed a long, tired sigh.

The distinguished author closed his eyes and fondly imagined the rambling route he was about to take through the moonlit London streets to his lodgings in Doughty Street, when he was aroused from his reverie by a less-than-polite *A-HEM*.

'Mr Dickens?' asked a gruff voice. The great man looked up, his bushy eyebrows rising and a half-smile playing on his lips.

Standing before him were two tall silhouettes that cast huge, hulking shadows against the back of the closed stage curtain. 'Mr *Charles* Dickens?'

The celebrated author nodded and wearily began to rise from his chair. *Autograph hunters*, he thought, *they most likely have a copy of* Oliver Twist *or* The Old Curiosity Shop *that they would like me to sign*. He sighed once again. *Well, no matter; I am always happy to sign the odd book for a loyal admirer of my work.*

He was reaching for the quill that lay beside an inkpot on the lectern when, to his astonishment, his wrist has grabbed quite roughly by one of the massive men.

'You're coming with us, Dickens,' said the first man, a snarl in his voice. Charles Dickens' grey, bushy eyebrows rose further, and he tried to pull his arm back from the thug's vice-like grip.

'Heh heh,' giggled the second man with a nasal laugh, 'Old Charlie's being *kitten-and-cat-flapped*, Mr Grimble, ain't he?'

'*Kitten-and-cat-flapped, Mr Bleat?*' said Mr Grimble, with a raised bushy eyebrow. '*Kidnapped*, Mr Grimble,' replied Mr Bleat.

The Diary of Master Abraham Stoker

Thursday 23rd of July 1859

19 Buckingham Street, Dublin

Dearest Diary,

Well, my old friend, the day is almost here. Tomorrow morning I will embark on a brand-new adventure — I shall, for the first time in my twelve years, leave the country of my birth and travel to another. Isn't it simply thrilling?

Goodbye to the Reverend Woods' famously boring school; farewell to dreary old Dublin; and good riddance to 19 Buckingham Street! At least, farewell, goodbye and good riddance for a few days.

The next time I write in your pages, my most Dearest Diary, I shall be *en route* to LONDON!

At six o'clock in the morning I shall rise and dress and breakfast, and then Mama, Papa and I will travel to Kingstown by carriage to catch the half-past-eight steam packet to Holyhead. There we will board a train bound for the biggest and most important city in the world with the express mission of retrieving my older brother Thornley from his end-of-term at

Withering Hall boarding school and bringing him home to dear old Dublin for the summer holidays.

And if that isn't exciting enough, Dear Diary, my parents and I will not make a mere party-of-three — much to my surprise and delight, Mama has said I may bring a guest, and I have selected whom else but my best friend and fellow adventurer ... Miss Molly Malone!

Oh, Diary, I find myself practically vibrating with excitement and shivering with anticipation! I have long desired to become a writer, and where better to find stories to tell and adventures to be had than the greatest city in the whole, wide world — London!

Until we speak, or should I say *write*, again,

Your friend,

Bram.

CHAPTER ONE:

SO LONG, FAREWELL, I BID YOU ALL ADIEU

IN WHICH MOLLY BIDS THE SPOOKS A FOND FAREWELL.

'It was the best of rhymes!' exclaimed Billy the Pan indignantly.

'It was the worst of rhymes,' said Hetty Hardwicke with a sniff. 'You couldn't even call it a poem – it barely rhymed at all – who rhymes *Her Majesty* with *too scratchity*?'

'I liked it, Billy,' said Rose.

'Yeah, me too,' said Shep. 'Read it again!'

Billy stood in the centre of Madame Flo's velvet-lined sitting room and took out the crumpled piece of paper from the pocket of his ragged jacket. He looked around at his audience, cleared his throat and removed the saucepan from his head for extra respectful gravitas. Shep nodded his head encouragingly at his friend.

'*A Powem on de Hawliday of Moly Malowne to Lundun,*' read Billy out loud in as deep a voice as he could muster, '*by ree-nowned pikpokket, rispectid member of the Brudderhud of Beggarmen –*'

'And Beggarwomen!' interjected Rose, who never liked to see girls left out. Hetty snorted a scornful snort.

'*And Beggarwimmen,*' continued Billy, darting a peeved look at Hetty, '*and prowd member of de faymus Dubblin gang, de Sakvill Strete Spoockes … me, Billy the Pan.*'

'Get on with it, you lanky eejit,' jeered Hetty.

Billy the Pan cleared his throat again and, raising his saucepan in the air, read out his poem.

O, deerist Moly
  Wee will mizz yew soe
  As awf to Lundun
  Yew wil goe
Furst on de boawt
  Den by de rayle
  Wit owr frend Bram
  Yew wil set sayle
Have a gud tyme in Lundun
  With Bram and Hur Matchisty
  I hope dat hur flees
  Don't get too scratchity.

'And another thing,' said Hetty, 'Her Majesty doesn't even *have* fleas anymore! Molly keeps her dog nice and clean.'

'Which is more than can be said for *your* dog,' said Billy. 'Prince Albert's got so many fleas, his fleas have fleas.'

'Face it, Billy,' snarled Hetty, 'You're about as good at poetry as you are at pick-pocketing!'

'Well, I …' said a voice from behind them, '… LOVED it!'

'MOLLY!' exclaimed Rose and Shep in unison as they ran to their friend and hugged her.

'As it happens, Her Majesty actually still has a couple of fleas,' said Molly, glaring at Billy and Hetty, who didn't notice Molly's glare as they were too busy glaring at each other. 'I just hope they aren't charged the full ticket price on the boat!'

Her Majesty, Molly's beloved knee-high, brown-furred, floppy-eared, floppy-tongued mutt sniffed loudly and licked Molly's knee to show that she took no offence.

'Just tell this scraggy dimwit here to leave Prince Albert out of it,' said Hetty, her voice rising in outrage. 'Prince Albert might have more fleas than Her Majesty, but at least he doesn't wear a stupid saucepan on his head!'

'Ah, Hetty,' said Rose. 'You know Billy has to wear that saucepan for work, it makes him stand out from all the other beggarmen – punters rap on the side of the pot for luck and then give him a ha'penny – it's how he makes his living.'

'Besides that,' said Billy, polishing his slightly rusty saucepan with a very dirty jacket sleeve and placing it back on his head, 'I think it makes me look very fashionable.'

Molly sighed and rolled her eyes. 'Shep,' she said, 'did you have any luck getting me a travelling trunk?'

'Yes!' said Shep and eagerly pushed a large table-cloth-covered rectangular shape into the centre of the room. 'Madame Flo borrowed it from her pal, The Marvellously Mystical Michelangelo Malvolio – you know him, his patch is three down from Flo's fortune-telling tent in Smithfield Carnival.'

'Ah, yeah,' smiled Molly, 'Magic Mick! How is the flamboyant old fraud?'

'He's grand, Mol,' replied Shep. 'He said to say thanks very much for the favour you did for you-know-who about the who-knows-what, that time they got stuck in the you-know-where – he said you'd know what he was talking about.'

Molly nodded, but to be honest, she couldn't quite remember what favour she had done for Magic Mick – she did so many good deeds for so many people that she had a hard time keeping track of all of them. But doing favours for people meant that they, in turn, owed *her* a favour. And the favour she asked from Magic Mick was one that only a magician could perform.

Rose bounced to her feet and, with a very magician-like 'Ta-daaa!' swished the patterned tablecloth off the rectangular shape. It was a big red travelling trunk with a curved lid. The trunk was tall – the top of the lid came up to Rose's chest – and its sides were festooned with labels and triangular stickers: some that read Buenos Aires, others reading New York, Glasgow and Oslo; there was even one that read Kathmandu. According to the labels, this huge travelling case has seen a great deal of travel. Rose opened the catch with a soft KLIKK and lifted the lid. 'It's big because Magic Mick hides his assistant in there during his act,' she said.

'Plus, two turtledoves, five hamsters, seven rabbits and a Norwegian Blue parrot,' added Shep.

Molly came closer for a better look. In the lid of the trunk were compartments for toiletries – toothbrush, washcloths, hairbrush and so on. There was a pull-out drawer for boots, and another for books (Molly had specifically requested the book drawer). The inside of the trunk looked very normal; Rose had neatly laid out some of Molly's petticoats and dresses, and they seemed to completely fill the trunk's interior.

'Janey Mack, Rose,' said Billy the Pan, 'how many dresses do you think Molly will be wearin' in London? That trunk is massive and it's full to the brim – she's only goin' for a week!'

'Ahhh,' said Rose, 'the trunk *does* look full up, but this is no ordinary travellin' trunk – right, Shep?'

Shep nodded. 'Yep,' he agreed, 'this trunk was made by the Marvellously Mystical Michelangelo Malvolio himself – just look at this!' He reached out his hands to both sides of the trunk and pressed two tiny hidden buttons, then, with a flourish and a cry of 'Abra-ka-boouushh!' he whipped out a wooden tray that held Molly's dresses – the dresses were stacked four-deep and wobbled as he held it high in the air. The tray had stretched from one side of the box to the other and had completely concealed a large space underneath.

Molly's eyes widened. 'It's like a dog kennel!' she said, walking around the trunk and peering in. 'It's got a little doggy bed, a built-in bowl, it's even got a holder on the side with a tiny toy bear in it!'

'That's just in case Her Majesty gets bored while she's on her journey; I asked Magic Mick for that meself,' said Shep proudly. At the mention of her name, Her Majesty jumped up and laid her shaggy paws the side of the trunk, trying to look in too.

'No, no,' said Rose, 'you don't get in that way, girl.' She reached down to the back of the trunk, peeled back one of the triangular destination labels (fittingly, it read *LONDON*) and pressed a button that was hidden behind the sticker. Immediately a dog-sized door at the trunk's side swung silently open.

'Welcome to your new home, Her Majesty,' said Shep with a low bow. Grinning a doggy grin, the Sackville Street Spook's beloved mutt trotted though the little door and into the trunk. She settled herself down on her new dog bed with a wide, satisfied yawn and gave the toy bear a friendly sniff.

'It's perfect!' proclaimed Molly. 'Well done, Shep!' The small boy's face lit up with pride and pleasure.

'I don't know why you have to bring your dog with you to London, anyway,' said Hetty. 'It seems like an awful lot of fuss.'

'Dog-nappers,' said Molly, 'that's why. A couple of eejits tried to rob Her Majesty when I left her tied up outside Mulligan's fishmongers last week – I'm not lettin' her out of my sight ever again after that.'

'Don't worry, Hetty,' said Billy the Pan, 'them dog-nappers wouldn't be bothered to take Prince Albert; he's just too pug-ugly.' Hetty furrowed her thick eyebrows and growled at Billy, sounding just like her dog.

'Enough!' said Molly, standing up. 'I'll be gone for five days, and business will have to go on as usual while I'm away.' She furrowed her eyebrows and looked at the Spooks: red-haired Rose in her faded blue dress and tattered pinafore; little Shep with his tight, jet-black curly hair and his dribbly nose even wetter than Her Majesty's; then there was wiry-haired Hetty with her own dog on a rope; and lastly, skinny, long-limbed Billy with his ridiculous sauce-pan hat. *Hmmmm, time to choose …*

Hetty was whip-smart and knew the back alleys, lanes and cobblestone passageways of Dublin like the back of her grimy hand; but she had a big mouth and, what was worse, a sharp tongue – either of which could land the Sackville Street Spooks in a big heap of trouble.

Billy was older and had been with Molly's gang of underage pickpockets and sneak thieves for longer than anyone. Maybe he wasn't the shiniest fork in the cutlery drawer, but he was brave and loyal, and, most importantly, people liked him. And where prickly Hetty sometimes behaved like a porcupine in a balloon factory, Billy tended to have a light touch – and a light touch was a pickpocket's best weapon …

'Billy,' said Molly, her mind made up, 'I'm leavin' you in charge while I'm in London.' Out of the corner of her eye she could see Hetty opening her cavernous mouth, a look of outrage spreading across her slightly grubby face. 'Hetty, you're second in command,' said Molly quickly. 'You're the best yapper I know; there's a lot you can teach the younger ones about talking your way out of sticky situations.'

Hetty's open gob closed with a KLOPP; she wrinkled her nose, but looked mostly mollified by Molly's words. 'I s'pose second in command is better than third,' she said and flomped down onto Madame Flo's threadbare sofa.

Molly sighed a silent sigh. 'No time for sitting down, Hetty,' she said in a cheery voice. 'C'mon, lads, let's get this tricked-out travellin' trunk on the back of the carriage – we have to be in Kingstown by eight o'clock!'

* * *

An hour and a half later, after crossing the River Liffey at Carlisle Bridge and the Dodder at Balls Bridge, and following the coast road through Booterstown, Williamstown and Blackrock, the horse-drawn carriage carrying the Sackville Street Spooks – and a travelling trunk containing Her Majesty – pulled up at the gate to Kingstown Harbour's East Pier.

As Billy, Hetty and Shep carefully unloaded the trunk off the carriage and onto a porter's barrow, Rose and Molly gazed at the massive hulk of the *PS Hibernia* moored at the side of the wharf, with its gangplank down and passengers lining up to board. The sides of the wooden paddle steamer were painted red and gold, and in the centre a tall white chimney belched grey smoke from its black-painted cap. Fore and aft of the chimney were three tall masts and in the rigging the ship's crew were busy unfurling wide white calico sails. Either side of the ship were two enormous, powerful-looking steam-driven paddle wheels, both of which seemed to be quivering with energy and anticipation for the voyage ahead.

'This is where I leave yiz,' said Molly to the Spooks, 'Look after each other, and try not to get into *too* much trouble!'

'No worries, Mol,' said Shep, then whispered, 'an' don't worry about Hetty and Billy; me an' Rose will stop them two eejits from eatin' each other alive!'

Billy wiped his eyes with a filthy sleeve and, snorting back a sniffle, rapped on the side of the travelling trunk. From deep within, Her Majesty barked back a muffled *woof*.

CHAPTER 2

WAVES, TRAINS AND ROUND CARRIAGE WHEELS

IN WHICH MOLLY AND BRAM SET SAIL FOR WALES, AND GO LOCO FOR LONDON

'Ah, Molly,' said Bram, looking at his gold-plated pocket watch, 'you're right on time!' Molly waved a hand in greeting to Bram's parents as she strolled towards the gangplank. A red-faced porter huffed and puffed noisily behind her, pulling her enormous travelling trunk along on his trolley; he shook his head and grunted sharply as he began to push the barrow up the incline of the gangplank onto the ship.

'I see you've brought, ahem, a large wardrobe with you, my dear,' said Bram's mother, eyeing the trunk. 'What a clever girl; I do *so* approve – the weather in London is *so* changeable and it is *so* important that one provides oneself with options for *every* occasion.'

Bram hid a smile behind his hand and hugged his friend. 'Isn't this wonderful, Mol?' he grinned, 'I know you've been to New York, but I've never even left Ireland before – I am sure we shall have a simply splendid time in jolly old London!'

Molly turned to Bram's parents. 'Thank you *so* much for inviting me to come,' she said, using the most high-pitched, upper-crust voice she could muster. 'I am *so* looking forward to visiting the city and seeing *all* the sights – Buckingham Palace, the British Museum, even the Tower of London where people got their heads chopped off!'

'Hrrumph,' said Papa Stoker.

'You are most welcome, Miss Malone,' said Bram's mother. 'It will be good for Bram to have someone to explore with!' She leaned in close to Molly and squeezed her arm affectionately. 'And don't worry about having to use your, a-hem, upper-class accent around me, Molly,' she whispered with a wink. 'Bram has told me all about the *real* Miss Malone.'

Molly shot Bram a look. 'Sorry, Mol,' he said quietly. 'You couldn't pretend to be the wayward ward of a wealthy landowner for the whole trip. And besides that, your put-on plummy voice was driving me to absolute distraction.'

As they began to board the ship, Bram pointed ahead towards the red-faced porter who had just reached the top of the gangplank with Molly's trunk. 'I thought you said you didn't trust porters with your travelling trunk,' he whispered.

'I don't,' replied Molly quietly, 'but it turns out it's a little too heavy to carry myself.'

'Too heavy?' hissed Bram. 'Mol, how could your trunk be too heavy? All I brought was a change of clothes and two books to read on the train – my diary and my copy of *A Christmas Carol*, the one Charles Dickens signed for me when we met him. What on earth are *you* bringing to London?'

Before Molly could answer, a haughty and imperious voice sounded from behind them.

'Steward,' it snapped, its tone upper-class and as sharp as a razor, 'the gangplank is obstructed – kindly move these riff-raff out of my way, I demand to board immediately!' The deep voice belonged to a tall, broad-shouldered woman who barged past the Stokers in a very brusque manner. The woman was dressed head to toe in black – her dress was black lace; her large bustle at the back was black; her overcoat and hat were black; even the veil she wore over her face was black. Despite the veil, Molly could see that the woman's head was held at an angle that seemed to be suggesting that her well-bred nostrils were, at that very moment, being forced to smell something (or someone) rather unsavoury. She carried a silver-topped blackthorn cane that swished savagely as she walked.

The Ship's Steward who tip-toed along in her wake gulped a quiet gulp. 'At once, Lady H,' he said, and then, with an apologetic look, addressed the Stoker party. 'I am so sorry,' he stuttered, 'Lady H has paid extra for premium first-class passage.'

'I say,' said Bram. 'Papa has booked first-class tickets for us too!'

'Ah,' said the Steward with a pained expression as he padded up the gangplank in the snooty Lady's wake. 'Lady H's tickets are *premium* first-class, she booked them for herself, and her travelling companion.' A young boy in uniform trotted behind the Steward. He held a black rectangular cage with metal bars on three sides; inside the cage was a large, fluffy white cat.

'Her name's Estella,' said the boy to Molly and Bram as they boarded the steamer. 'The cat, I mean, not her Ladyship.'

'Hrrumph,' said Papa Stoker, 'buying first-class tickets for a cat? And *premium* ones at that, if you please?' He straightened his bowler hat and HRRUMPHed again. 'Some people have more money than sense.'

Onboard, once the porters had secured their cases and travelling trunks, Molly and the Stokers found themselves sitting outdoors in the first-class section of the deck, on wooden benches directly opposite the haughty figure of Lady H, who sat with her caged feline companion beside her. As the great paddles began to turn, the woman gazed disdainfully out to sea, her face obscured by the black veil that covered it.

'If she has premium tickets,' whispered Bram to Molly, 'why is she sitting on the same wooden seats as us?'

Molly grinned. 'Look closer – under her bustle,' she said to her friend, 'the only difference between first-class and *premium* first-class is that stuck-up Lady H there has a cushion under her bum!'

Bram giggled quietly, while Lady H kept her gaze fixedly away from the 'riff-raff' Stokers. 'Look at her,' he whispered to Molly, 'sitting there, in the same sunshine as we are, with her nose in the air – that's nothing but daylight snobbery!'

The morning was bright and sunny, and the sea was as calm and smooth as the deep green water in the Royal Canal. While Bram's father settled down to do the crossword and Mama Stoker read a book, Molly and Bram went for a wander around the steamer and to watch Howth Head and the smoky Dublin skyline as it disappeared into the distance.

When they drew close to the covered section of the deck where the passengers' luggage was stored, Molly grabbed Bram by the arm. 'Err, Bram, ol' buddy, ol' pal,' she said, grinning her most disarming grin, 'I may have a little bit of a confession to make.' Bram raised an eyebrow at his "ol' pal".

'Mol, what have you done?' he asked with a faint note of alarm in his voice.

'Well,' said Molly, 'you know how your parents kindly said you could take a plus-one on the trip?'

'Yeesssss,' said Bram. He wasn't sure he liked where this conversation was going.

'And you remember how happy you were to ask me along,' said Molly, 'and how happy I was to be asked?' She slapped the palm of her hand on the top of her sticker-covered travelling trunk; there was the sound of movement from inside.

Bram took a step back. 'Oh no, Mol,' he said, his voice trembling, 'you haven't brought all of the Sackville Street Spooks with you? They aren't all squeezed into that trunk, are they?'

'Not *all* of them,' replied Molly, her eyes twinkling, 'just the furry one. She's never been to

London before either, and I thought she'd enjoy the trip!'

'Her Majesty?!' whispered Bram in astonishment, 'Your *dog* is in your trunk?' He got down on his knees. 'Is she alright in there?'

'Ah, she's been in tighter spots than that,' grinned Molly. 'I'm sure she's fine – have a look for yourself!'

While Molly kept watch, Bram peered in through the small breathing holes that Magic Mick had thoughtfully drilled into the sides of the trunk. A long, wet tongue poked out through one of the holes and licked Bram's nose. 'I *think* she's alright,' he said over his shoulder to Molly, wiping his face with a pocket handkerchief, 'but, Mol, how are we going to keep her a secret from Mama and Papa? If they find out we've brought a dog with us, they might send *me* to the Tower of London!'

He got to his feet again, but to his surprise Molly wasn't there. He looked around and found her at the other side of the pile of leather-bound suitcases, trunks and other assorted pieces of luggage, leaning against a metal railing and chatting to the Ship's Boy. 'Ah, Bram,' she said, 'this is Dafydd; he was just tellin' me all about that sour-faced aul banshee who pushed past us in the queue – the mysterious Lady H.'

'That's the thing, you see,' said the boy, 'she *is* mysterious – nobody knows anything about Lady H, not even what the "*H*" stands for. They say she dresses all in black because she suffered a terrible tragedy twenty years ago.'

'Oh,' said Molly, 'did someone belongin' to her die?'

'If someone did die,' said Bram, 'it must have been someone she cared a lot about, like a family member or a really close friend – she's still in mourning dress today!'

'The only "friend" I've ever seen her with is her cat, Estella,' said Dafydd, 'and she doesn't even seem to like *her* very much. She keeps her locked up in that tiny cage and walks about with it on her arm like she's carrying a fancy handbag from Paris. I've never seen her pet the poor cat or pay it any attention at all, the unfortunate thing. It's pitiful.'

Molly thought of her own pet, Her Majesty. She loved that dog like a member of her family – in fact, since Molly was an orphan, Her Majesty *was* part of her actual family. Molly was always hugging the dog and showering her with affection, just like all the Sackville Street Spooks did, and she hated to be parted from her – that was part of the reason she was smuggling Her Majesty to London for her holiday. Molly hated the thought of any animal being mistreated, imprisoned or, worse, ignored – especially by a snooty, old, black-covered crow like Lady H.

'She usually travels with two big man-servants, does Lady H,' continued Dafydd, 'great, big lummoxes they are. They speak in that London riddle-talk, you know, the kind that rhymes.'

'Oh, yes,' said Bram 'you mean *climbing gang*.'

'*Climbing gang?*' asked the boy.

'*Rhyming slang,*' said Bram, 'I've read about this – Londoners sometimes disguise what they're talking about by substituting a rhyme for a word or phrase, rather than using the word itself – so *climbing gang* becomes *rhyming slang*. Most people use it just for fun, but some people, especially the criminal elements, use it to evade being caught out by the police! It can be devilishly hard to crack their code at times, though,' added Bram. 'They'll say things like, *"Fancy a cup of fig?"'*

'A cup of *what* now?' said Molly, perplexed.

'A *cup of fig*,' said Bram, '*fig* is short for *fig tree, tree* rhymes with *tea*, so what they actually mean is, *"Fancy a cup of TEA?"'*

Molly shook her head in exasperation. 'London,' she said, 'it's a whole other country.'

* * *

Seagulls wheeled in lazy circles in the sky as the *PS Hibernia* chugged into Holyhead Port, its big paddle wheels slowing and the crew climbing the rigging once again to lower the sails. Molly, Bram and the Stokers disembarked to find the two o'clock train waiting for them in the nearby station, and while Papa Stoker went about the business of locating their luggage onboard the paddle steamer and having the porters transfer it to the mail carriage of the steam train, the two children were given the job of locating a suitable passenger compartment for the family's long rail journey to London.

They walked along the platform admiring the huge steam train. The metal engine was long and painted a shiny black, with a smoking chimney at the front and an open-air cab at the rear where the driver stood. Behind that was a tender from which the fireman shovelled coal into the engine's firebox to create the steam that drove the train's huge steel wheels, and attached to the coal tender was a mail carriage, followed by four passenger carriages. 'That poor driver will get soaked if it rains,' said Molly, 'but I suppose if he gets wet, he always has the firebox to warm his backside up again!'

'Those were my first footsteps in a new country, Mol,' said Bram as he hopped off the platform and up into a passenger carriage. He yawned and stretched his arms wide. 'Now we need to find some nice seats where we can sit down, and I can rest my poor feet!'

'But not *these* seats,' said Molly, as they passed a compartment in which Lady H was sitting, her face obscured by the black veil and her bony hands resting on her silver-topped cane. 'I think the atmosphere might be a bit frosty in that compartment!'

The next compartment along was unoccupied, and Molly and Bram quickly sat at the window, facing each other on red velvet seats.

'Ah, *there* you are, children,' said Mama Stoker as she and Bram's father joined them. 'Is everything alright, Miss Malone?'

Molly was frowning. 'Oh, yes, I think so, Mrs Stoker,' she said, 'I just can't help feeling that I've forgotten something.'

At the stroke of two o'clock, the guard blew a shrill PEEEEEP on his whistle. There was an answering TOOT-TOOOOOT from the driver's whistle in the engine's cab, and the train slowly shuddered into motion. Soon they were CHUGG-CHUGGing along the rails towards London, and Bram's parents had settled back to their crosswords and books.

Molly looked out the window, watching the Welsh landscape go by, while Bram took out his Dickens book and began to re-read it for what Molly thought must be the twenty-seventh time. She sat back in her comfortable seat and thought about her younger days, back when she was a part-time pickpocket, running from the Peelers with her friends, the Sackville Street Spooks. *They are more than friends*, thought Molly, *Billy, Rose, Shep, Calico Tom – even Hetty – they are my family*. Molly had been born in the North Dublin Workhouse and had never known her own mother and father. Once she had been old enough to ask about them, the guards in the workhouse – the inmates called them turnkeys – had told her that her parents had died shortly after she was born. 'They took one look at you and kicked the bucket,' said one particularly cruel guard with a sadistic laugh. Molly had packed up her few possessions that night and escaped the workhouse, climbing over the tall stone wall in the November moonlight and landing on the cobblestones on the other side without a ha'penny to her name, but *free*.

Wandering alone in the cold Dublin Streets, she had found herself in bustling Smithfield Market. The fair was on that day and the Square was heaving with people and farmers buying and selling animals of all sorts – pigs, sheep, cows, geese, goats and ponies were changing hands – the crowds were crushing, and the noise was deafening. Molly had taken refuge from the mayhem in an alleyway off the square where she came across a lanky boy trying to defend a scraggy-looking, starving pup from bigger boys who wanted to bully it. The boy was wearing what seemed to be a saucepan of some variety on his head and was waving a broken broom handle ineffectually in the direction of the bully-boys, who returned his entreaties to 'Leave the poor little mutt alone,' with scornful laughter. Having just escaped the workhouse, Molly had had quite enough of bullies herself. Drawing herself to her full height, she marched past the poor puppy's lanky protector, whipping the saucepan from his head, raising it high in the air and KLONKKing it straight down on the nearest hooligan's head. The ruffian hit the floor and the other boys, unnerved by the sight of their leader being bested by a young girl in a grubby Workhouse uniform, turned their tails and fled.

'Thanks for helpin',' said the lanky boy as Molly handed him back his saucepan headgear. 'I'm Billy.'

But Molly was only half-listening, she was on her knees hugging and petting the scrawny, shivering puppy. 'I'm Molly,' she said. 'What's the dog called?'

The ragged boy shook his head and shrugged his bony shoulders; he didn't know.

'Well then, girl,' said Molly to the little puppy as it happily licked her face and hands. 'I'll think of a name for you, but in the meantime, I'm goin' to treat you like *royalty*.'

'Do you know, Mol,' said Bram putting down his book, 'modern trains can travel at speeds of up to forty miles an hour? FORTY MILES AN HOUR! I have never dreamed I should be travelling so fast! Why, at this speed we shall be in London by this evening!'

Molly took a familiar-looking gold-plated pocket watch from the small lace handbag that lay beside her on the seat and began to wind it. Bram looked quizzically at the watch – he didn't know Molly possessed one – and then patted his own pockets as realisation dawned on him.

'Don't worry, Bram,' said Molly with a wink, 'I only borrowed it!' She tossed it back to him. 'C'mon, Quality,' she said, grinning at the look of bewilderment on his face, 'this locomotive journey seems simply endless – let's go for a stroll along the corridor an' stretch our legs.'

Before Bram could answer, Molly had opened the compartment door and was striding purposefully up the passageway. Bram flashed his parents a smile and followed her.

Molly had reached the end of the corridor and was looking out the window of the carriage door towards the next coach along. The next carriage was attached by big, round metal couplings and, looking down, Bram could see wooden railway sleepers racing by underneath the train as the steam engine barrelled along the steel tracks.

'Molly, I don't think we —' he started to say, but Molly had already opened the door and was gingerly hopping over the couplings onto the footplate of the next carriage. The thundering noise of the train engine filled Bram's ears and he nervously stepped across the gap as quickly as he could, trying his best not to look down at the speeding sleepers and oil-stained gravel below, as grit from the tracks got into his eyes and the strong wind blew back his hair.

'This is the mail coach,' shouted Molly over the CHUCKKETTA-CHUCKKETTA noise of the train. 'I just remembered what I forgot to do — I forgot to check on Her Majesty! She's in there all alone; I just want to peep in the window an' make sure she's okay!'

Clinging to the mail coach's door handle, Molly rubbed soot off the window and peered in. 'It's dark in there,' she shouted back to Bram, 'but I can see Her Majesty's trunk, all safe and sound.'

Bram wiped soot from his eyes. 'Great!' he spluttered. 'Can we go back in now?'

'An' she's not alone in there either,' said Molly, 'I can see Lady H's poor little cat, Estella, in there too. Ah, Bram, she's up on a high shelf, still stuck in her cage! Poor thing; at least Her Maj is only locked up until we get to London, that miserable creature is a full-time prisoner – she's always in the slammer.'

Molly hopped nimbly back across the gap, and she and Bram slipped back through the door into the safety of the first passenger carriage. 'Holy moly, Molly,' said Bram, looking at his friend, 'we better visit the washroom before we go back to Mama and Papa, you look very much like Welsh coal miner!' Both their faces were covered in smears of soot from standing on the train's footplate, and their clothes were smudged and blackened from the engine's black smoke. Molly looked down at herself and started to smile. 'It reminds me of what I used to dress like, Bram,' she giggled, 'back when I was a full-time pickpocket! You look like a street urchin now too, your clothes are so dirty – you don't look much like quality at all now, Quality!'

As they walked down the corridor towards the washroom, leaving sooty footprints behind them, they found their way blocked by a broad-shouldered shape who was walking up and down the corridor, reading a book. 'Lady H,' whispered Molly to Bram.

Bram looked at the title on the book's spine and then up to the blacked veiled face of the book's owner. 'A-ha,' he said cheerily, 'You're reading *The Old Curiosity Shop*, Madam!' He took out his signed copy of *A Christmas Carol* from the pocket of his jacket and held its slightly sooty cover up to her, 'I am a huge admirer of Mr Charles Dickens too. *The Old Curiosity Shop* is a really lovely book!'

'If I require a book review from a … a *chimney-sweep*,' said Lady H icily from behind her veil, 'I will ask for it. Good day!' With that, she entered her compartment, slamming the door behind her.

Molly and Bram looked at each other's grubby, soot-covered faces and burst into giggles again.

'A coal miner and a chimney-sweep,' chortled Molly.

'Two good, honest jobs,' replied Bram. 'Right-ho, guv-nah!' said Molly in a mock-Cockney accent, and they chuckled and guffawed their way down to the washroom.

CHAPTER THREE

MAYBE IT'S BECAUSE I'M A DUBLINER ...

IN WHICH MOLLY AND BRAM TOUR A TOWER AND PEER AT SOME PICKPOCKETS

It was dark by the time the train pulled into the platform at London's Euston Station and the London streets were foggy. Molly and Bram, tired from the travelling, were happy enough to hear that

Mama and Papa Stoker had decided that they would all head directly towards their hotel for dinner and an early night.

'We can go sight-seeing in the morning,' said Bram with a yawn as he helped his father find a porter to bring their luggage, and Molly's huge travelling trunk, to a waiting hansom cab. 'London will still be here.' Molly climbed up into the cab and drowsily stared out at the grand façade of the train station, in front of which a muscle-bound manservant was heaving a great load of bags and cases onto the back of a horse-drawn carriage. Lady H, with Estella's cage on her knee, glared back at Molly from the carriage's window. Molly stuck out her tongue at the snooty woman, then sat back in her seat and watched the rows of gas lamps that illuminated the streets as best they could through the heavy fog as the Stoker's cab made its way to their hotel. *My first view of London*, she thought sleepily as the carriage clattered over cobblestones, *and I'm too tired to look properly.*

The Diary of Master Abraham Stoker
Friday 24th of July 1859

51

The Great Northern Hotel, London

Dearest Diary,

Greetings from jolly old London!

It was a long journey – a VERY long journey – but we are now safely ensconced in our well-appointed hotel. The cab driver who brought us here was very apologetic about the fog; 'A real pea-souper, sir, if you catch my drift,' he said to my father (who, it has to be said, didn't quite catch the cab driver's drift), 'but it shall be cleared up by morning, just you see, sir!' I do hope he was right; the fog tonight was so thick that one couldn't see one's hand in front of one's face, no matter how vigorously one waggled one's fingers!

The hotel is a fine establishment at King's Cross, and Papa has retained three rooms on the fourth floor; Mama and Papa have a large room that comes with every modern convenience one can imagine – a chaise longue for Mama to read on, a writing desk for Papa, it even has a bath! Molly and I are across the hallway in two adjoining rooms, connected by a door so we can pop in and out of each other's room as we please.

Though quite worn out, Molly managed to liberate Her Majesty from the hiding hole at the bottom of her travelling trunk and now, fed on biscuits and some fresh water from a wash basin, the poor animal is safe and sound, sleeping under Molly's bed. A bed in which, if the snores I can hear through the connecting door are anything to go by, Molly is fast asleep.

And now I'm afraid I find that I am so trembling with tiredness and fatigue, I can hardly hold my pencil to write; I think it may be high time to take some rest myself.

I look forward to seeing the city tomorrow morning – if, of course, the driver's weather forecasting abilities prove to be correct, and the 'pea-soup' fog clears up! Our first stop is to be the Houses of Parliament, where Father has some Dublin Castle correspondence to deliver on behalf of the Lord Lieutenant. Papa was grumbling (he's always grumbling!) that just because he's a civil servant doesn't mean that old Carlisle should be able to treat him as a messenger boy – he's the la-di-da Keeper of the Crown Jewels, don't-cha know, and he IS on holidays after all – but the Lord Lieutenant's Office has arranged for us to have a tour of the new clock tower they have built beside Parliament, I suppose with the aim of keeping us amused while Papa is busy, so it all seems to be working out for the best. I'd quite like to bump into the Prime Minister while we are there – Molly says he's an absentee landlord and an absolute rotter, and says if she meets him, she'll give him a hefty kick in the rear end. THAT I would LOVE to see!

I will report on our adventures again, Dear Diary, in due course – if I can keep Mol out of gaol ...

Your friend,

Bram.

The next morning, following a hearty breakfast of cold meats, cheese, milk and tea, Molly and Bram walked out into the London sunshine. 'Looks like the cab driver was spot-on with his weather prediction,' said Bram, 'it's turned out to be a simply splendid day!'

Another cab driver awaited them outside the hotel, and a top-hatted hotel doorman opened the carriage door for them and doffed his topper as they climbed in to join Bram's mother and father inside the cab.

'A quick tour of the new clock tower at Westminster Palace, I believe it is called St Stephen's Tower,' said Mama Stoker cheerily, 'and then the rest of the day is yours, children, to do with as you please!'

'Do you think,' said Molly, 'that they will let us into the Houses of Parliament and show us the cellar that Guy Fawkes packed with gunpowder when he tried to blow the place up?'

Mama Stoker laughed a snorting, somewhat unladylike laugh; she thought Molly had a wicked sense of humour.

Bram's father pointed out a few landmarks as the carriage clattered over cobblestones through the London streets towards Whitehall; most of the landmarks seemed to be monuments and statues – there seemed to be almost as many statues as there were people in the streets.

'The Empire does so love to pat itself on the back,' muttered Papa Stoker in his gruff voice. When they reached Tottenham Court Road, with its tall, white stone buildings and innumerable furniture shops, the carriage slowed down to a slow crawl due to the sheer number of people milling about and spilling off the pavements onto the road; there seemed to be *thousands* going about their business that morning. *My goodness*, thought Bram, *I should think that there are more people here in this one street in London than there are in the entirety of Ireland!*

Bram, always an avid people-watcher, studied as many faces as he could from the safety of the cab window. Wealthy gentlemen and ladies, *The Quality* as Molly called them – she used that nickname for Bram too – strode up and down at a stately speed in silk and satin finery, their silver canes swishing, and their noses held snootily in the air. Tradespeople, office clerks, workers and housewives dragging wailing children walked along at a quicker pace, their clothes clean but shabby and their eyes cast downwards. Lastly there were the lowest of the low, the poorest people that both the Quality and the waged class looked down on, if they deigned to look at all – the beggars and the destitute, sitting on the hard stone ground with their hands upraised.

Molly used to be part of this tribe; an orphan and a pickpocket who lived by her wits on the Dublin streets, one step away from the law and one break-fast away from starvation. She was clever, brave, loyal and a born leader. Bram was proud to call her his friend.

'Look!' said Molly in a half-whisper, pointing out the carriage window. 'There's our old pal!' A tall, broad-shouldered woman, dressed all in black, was striding down the pavement like a hot dagger sliding through a block of butter. The crowds were parting before her due to the guttural growls and angry bel-lows of warning emanating from the huge goon that shambled along beside her.

'Gerr-OW-dovvit!' he snarled, his muscle-bound arms pumping like locomotive pistons and his steam-powered eyebrows bristling. 'G-OW-on, SHIFFFT!' People were practically diving into the street at the sound of this menacing bark.

'Lady H!' said Bram. 'She's no friend of ours, though I wonder who *her* friend is?'

'I don't think I *want* to know,' said Molly. 'He looks like he's first cousin to a Yeti!'

The carriage passed down St Martin's Lane and then out into the broad expanse of Trafalgar Square.

'This Square was built to commemorate the Battle of Trafalgar,' said Mama Stoker, 'and if you look up to the top of that column, you might see another old friend of yours.'

'Oh! You mean *Nelson*, Mama,' said Bram, craning his neck out of the carriage window to survey the huge stone column that seemed to grow like a huge oak tree trunk from the dead centre of the Square. 'Oh yes, Horatio Nelson and I are old chums!'

'I prefer Nelson's Pillar in Dublin, meself,' said Molly. 'That has a viewing platform you can climb up to and look out over the city, this one's just a statue of an eejit, standin' doin' nuthin' on the top of a pole.' The size of the Square was impressive; so much bigger, Bram thought, than Smithfield Square in Dublin. It had two huge stone fountains, with cool water shooting skywards in the centre of each pool. Surrounding the Column itself on all four sides were four huge stone plinths.

'They should put something on those yokes,' said Molly, 'maybe statues of guard dogs.'

Bram nodded. 'They found skeletons of tigers and lions here when they were digging the foundations for the column, so maybe great big metal lions might be just the ticket.'

The driver guided his horses right at Charing Cross, the very centre of the city according to Londoners, and down onto Whitehall. As they passed the grand entrance to the Royal Horse Guards Parade, Molly leaned out of the carriage window and stuck out her tongue at two armour-clad cavalry soldiers wearing black tunics, white gloves and sashes, and helmets with long red tassels. Both were mounted on a huge, grey-dappled horse, and each held a shiny sword. 'Lookit yer man,' whispered Molly to Bram, pointing at one of the soldiers, 'his helmet looks like a coal scuttle!'

Turning left onto Bridge Street, the children could see the clean white blocks of the Houses of Parliament's new clock tower soaring high over the Parliament buildings, and, beside them, the bare, bony iron skeleton of the half-constructed Westminster Bridge, in the process of being built across the River Thames.

The cab was met at the lawn before the entrance to Parliament by two young gentlemen, each wearing a sharp black suit with tails, and each sporting a very impressive moustache.

'Mr Stoker,' said the first, in a voice as crisp as his starched white, wing-collared shirt, 'this way, if you please, sir.' He led Bram's father through stone gates and down some steps towards the entrance to Westminster Palace and the Houses of Parliament; Papa Stoker waved to Bram and Molly with one hand as he walked, clutching onto a small leather wallet of papers with the other.

'And Madam Stoker,' said the second young gentleman, 'if you and the children would like to follow me.' He made a clicking sound with the heels of his shoes and marched off toward the door to the new clock tower.

'He called me Madam,' said Mama Stoker as they trotted along after him, trying to catch up. 'Oh, Molly, does he really think I'm that old?'

'Don't mind him,' said Molly with a snort, 'you are a very fashionable lady, Mrs Stoker, with a very youthful attitude. He's just a jumped up, stiff-suited, snooty English eejit.'

Mrs Stoker giggled and linked Molly's arm. 'And

you, Molly, are a breath of fresh air; you must call me Charlotte from now on! I insist!'

They followed the stiff-suited eejit through the doors and into the Tower. 'This clock tower, known as St Stephen's Tower,' said the eejit in a very bored-sounding voice, 'was designed by Pugin and construction began in 1843, with the tower being officially completed in May of this year.' Although Bram was fascinated by the history of the Tower, Molly found herself being almost put to sleep by their tour guide's boring, droning voice. She and Mama Stoker trudged along behind the young gentleman, while Bram skipped happily beside him, peppering him with questions about the ornamental features and the types of stone used in the construction. Molly's interest was piqued when the guide showed them the small prison room at the base of the Tower; she had seen the inside of many gaol cells over the years and whispered to Bram that this one, with its oak panelled walls and leather-covered writing desk, was definitely the most well-appointed and upper-crust she had ever set eyes on. 'A *clink* for the Quality,' she said, miming hand-cuffs and sticking her nose snootily in the air.

'Now, Madam and young guests,' said the young gentleman guide, 'if you would like to step this way, we shall begin the ascent to the Clock Room.'

'The Clock Room?' said Mama Stoker in dismay. 'How many steps would that be?'

'There are two hundred and ninety steps to the Clock Room, Madam,' said the guide with a sniff, 'followed by forty-four to the Belfry.'

'My goodness,' said Mrs Stoker, 'what an awful lot of steps.'

'I'm afraid I haven't finished quite yet, Madam,' said the guide, one eyebrow raised. '*Then* we complete our climb with an additional fifty-nine steps to the Spire.'

'Oh dear,' whispered Mama Stoker to Molly, 'I'm not sure that my attitude, as youthful as you may think if to be, will be enough to get my old bones up quite that many steps – would you and Bram mind awfully if I sat this adventure out?'

With the tour guide walking before them, Molly and Bram began to climb the stone spiral staircase toward the Clock Tower. At each landing on the staircase were gas lamps and long, skinny stained-glass windows to let light in, and the two children stood on their tiptoes to take turns looking out the ones that were open to help air circulate in the tower, allowing them to see letterbox-shaped views of the city below them. 'Imagine what the view is going to be like from the Belfry!' said Bram.

They could hear the loud WHIRRRing and KLIKKing noises of the Clock Room long before they reached it, and the noise became deafening as they walked through the door into the room itself. The centre of the room was filled with a massive construction of steel and brass cogs of all sizes as well as huge wheels, various pulleys, a myriad of levers and a multitude of rods, all moving in unison as the clockwork TICKKed and TOCKKed in perfect, precise rhythm. At the middle of the mechanism was an immense swinging pendulum that disappeared into a hole in the wooden floor. Workers, each armed with metal cans of oil, darted here and there, applying generous drops of slippery oil to cogs and flywheels from their oilcans' long spouts.

'We use over fourteen gallons of oil a week,' roared the tour guide over the ear-splitting noise of the mechanism, 'to keep the clockwork running like, well, clockwork!'

The room was lit, not by gaslight like the stairwell was, but by sunlight that shone through the huge ivory-coloured circular clock faces that dominated each side of the room. As they watched, the shadow of the massive minute hand on the outside each clock face KLICKKed forward a minute.

'Thirty-seven minutes past eleven,' said Bram in wonder, reading the time in reverse through the immense coloured clock face glass.

'Think yourselves lucky that it's not five to twelve,' shouted the guide. 'We are to visit the Belfry next, and the sound of that big bell when it's rung on the hour should make your teeth rattle and your ears drop off!'

Forty-four steps later, Molly and Bram entered the Belfry of St Stephen's Tower. Four big iron bells hung from the ceiling of the Belfry on wooden beams, and in the centre hung the biggest bell either of the two friends had ever seen; to Bram it looked like the height of his three-storey childhood home in Marino Crescent. Thick ropes were tied to metal levers at the top of each bell, and they hung down to the wooden floor of the Belfry where they passed through holes that connected them to the clockwork mechanism below. Just then the ropes began to move jerkily up and down, seemingly of their own accord, and the four smaller bells started to sway. The ringers on each of the bells struck their sides, producing a sound that was extremely loud, yet melodious. Molly and Bram put their hands over their ears. 'The biggest bell,' shouted the guide over the pealing noise of the smaller bells, 'rings on the hour. It is the largest in London; although it hasn't been named as yet, it's new – it only rang out for the first time earlier this month – the workers just refer to it as the big bell.'

'Big Ben?' shouted Molly, her fingers in her ears. 'No, no,' shouted the guide, leading them towards the steps towards the Spire, 'it's called the big bell!'

'I think Big Ben is a much better name for that huge yoke than the big bell,' said Molly.

'I agree,' said Bram. 'I shall call it nothing else but Big Ben from this moment – although I'm not sure the name will catch on!'

The view from the Spire was breath-taking. Molly and Bram could see right across the River Thames to Lambeth Palace on the south bank, and all the way up the River to where it turned at Waterloo Bridge. The sun reflected prettily in the water as row boats, sail boats, barges and steamers, each as small as children's toys from where Molly and Bram were standing, moved lazily along it.

Looking from the east side of the Tower, the two friends had a view over the trees and grass of St James's Park to Buckingham Palace itself. 'There's a flag waving over the Palace portico!' said Bram, squinting into the distance and pointing. 'That means Queen Victoria herself is at home!'

At the mention of old Queen Vic, Molly remembered her half-joking plan to introduce Her Majesty to Her Majesty. 'Bram,' she said, 'this is all great fun, and the views are smashin', but I think I'd better head back to the hotel and get Her Majesty – I gave her to a nice chamber maid to look after, but the poor dog will be dyin' to get out and see London for herself!'

They thanked the tour guide, who looked happy enough to be getting rid of them, and skipped down the three hundred and ninety-four steps to the base of the Tower. Mama and Papa Stoker were waiting for them by the Prison Room, and they all walked out together into the warm summer sunshine.

'We are to travel to Withering Hall to collect Thornley this evening,' said Mrs Stoker to Bram. 'Papa and I will take tea now. You are, of course, more than welcome to join us.'

Bram shook his head. 'Thanks, Mama, but we have to go and visit an old friend.'

'An old friend?' said Mama, puzzled. 'In London? Bram, I didn't realise you knew anybody in London?'

'Don't worry, Charlotte,' said Molly with a laugh, 'he only means Her Majesty!' With a wave, the two friends trotted out the door of St Stephen's Tower in the direction of the River.

'Her *Majesty*?' said Mama to Papa Stoker. 'Oh, Abraham – you don't imagine the children are going to try to visit the *Queen*, do you?'

* * *

Molly and Bram strolled towards Westminster Bridge, the entrance to which was covered in wooden hoardings festooned with notices and various posters for circuses and theatre shows. Bram could see iron pilings sticking up from behind the hoarding and a couple of workers standing around, leaning on their shovels and looking like they were trying their best to avoid doing any actual work at all. Molly's attention was diverted by the sight of a small crowd of Londoners who had formed a circle around something sitting on the cobblestoned road beside the bridge. The object at the centre of the circle was making a loud, plaintive noise. 'AAAAAAAAHH-HHHHHHHHHHH!' it went, 'MAAAAAAAAMM-MAAAAAAAAAAAA!'

'Bram,' said Molly, 'listen to that wailing! If I'm not mistaken, I think we might be witnessin' the *Lost Baby* caper, or at least the London version of it!'

'I don't think you're mistaken, Mol,' said Bram, 'not in the least bit – it's most definitely the *Lost Baby* caper – look!' The crowd were gathered around what looked like a small child who was wearing a comically huge nappy. The child was emitting the loudest, most plaintive, most heart-breaking wail that Bram had ever heard. As Bram and Molly watched, three other children, their clothes ragged and their feet bare, seemed to appear from thin air. They were gliding in fluid, dance-like movements around and through the gathered crowd. Their small hands were darting in and out of people's pockets, relieving them of pocketbooks, pound notes and silk handkerchiefs, while the owners of said pocketbooks, pound notes and silk handkerchiefs were distracted by the titular and loudly-crying *Lost Baby*.

'This is how I first met you!' said Bram to Molly, 'Remember – at the Pillar in Sackville Street – Calico Tom was dressed up as the *Lost Baby* that time.'

All at once Molly and Bram noticed that the three wild children who had been dancing around the backs of the distracted crowd were suddenly nowhere to be seen, and that the loud wailing of the 'baby' had abruptly ceased. The crowd who had previously been looking at what they thought was an abandoned toddler sitting on the ground by the bridge were now looking around in puzzlement; some were scratching their heads and others, with looks of dawning shock and dismay, were checking their belongings – the baby was gone, and so had the contents of their pockets. A small shape sped past Molly and Bram, its grubby bare legs pumping up and down as it ran. It was holding a gold watch by its chain in one hand and seemed to be holding up its nappy with the other. ''Scuse me, Jimmy!' it cried as it flew by, a big, triumphant smile on its face.

'Well,' said Bram, looking at the tiny boy running pell-mell down the Strand, 'I think we may have just met the London version of Calico Tom!'

Chapter Four:

Extra! Read All About It!

In which Molly and Bram bring the dog for a stroll and learn some seriously shocking news

Once back at the Great Northern Hotel, Molly took Bram by the hand and led him around to the rear of the building towards the servant's entrance, which was situated in a dank and mouldering laneway. There was a strong smell of rotting food and vegetables that kitchen porters had thrown into a long row of rusty metal bins that lined the lane wall. Bram put up his hand to his nose to block the sour smell but Molly, well used to the soggy whiff of wet alleyways from her times with the Sackville Street Spooks – they regularly used them as escape routes when being chased by the Peelers – took a deep breath and sighed.

'Ahhhh!' she said. 'It smells like *home* to me; all big cities smell the same once you scratch the surface. Even out on the street you'll get the smell of smoke from the railways, the stink from the drains and the stench from the river,' said Molly. 'They say the Thames is so polluted, the locals call the water from it "monster soup"! Did you know,' she continued, rapping three times on the hotel's back door, one sharp knock and two softer ones, 'that during the *Great Stink* last year, the sewers all overflowed? Every sewer in London! It all seeped up through the manhole covers and flowed down the streets – the smell was terrible and people were slippin' around and fallin' all about in the poo-ey mess!'

Bram wrinkled his nose. 'Eww,' he said, 'that doesn't bear *stinking* about.'

The back door opened and there stood a young girl, holding Her Majesty by her lead. 'Thanks, Elsie!' said Molly, taking the leash and passing the maid a half crown coin. 'Oh, and thanks for brushing Her Majesty's fur, too – that green ribbon is a lovely touch!' Smiling, Elsie the chambermaid waved a goodbye and quietly closed the door. 'London has a huge population,' said Molly, giving Her Majesty a cuddle and a tickle under the chin, 'and a huge population can make an absolutely *humungous* smell!'

They walked back out onto Pancras Place and, while Bram studied a small street map, followed the road around onto Hamilton Place and then took a left onto Tonbridge Street. 'I'm really looking forward to seeing the British Museum this afternoon,' said Bram, looking up from his map and directing them right onto Cromer Street and then immediately left onto Hunter Street. 'I want to see the Rosetta Stone that scholars use to decipher Egyptian picture writing, and I believe they have some sculptures from the Parthenon in Greece, even though they're not meant to have them at all – the poor Greeks keep asking for them back, but the Museum keeps on telling them to take a hike.' He looked up from his map and smiled at Molly. 'It was so good of Mama and Papa to let us go to the Museum by ourselves, while they're at lunch.'

'I think your mother was more interested in fashion than she was in looking at dusty old stuff in a museum,' smiled Molly, 'and speakin' of that place in Greece, your Ma kept asking the waiter at breakfast for directions to somewhere called The Pantheon in Oxford Street. She told me it was full of beautiful dresses and fashionable boots and shoes.' Molly giggled. 'She wanted me to come with her this afternoon, but I told her *I* preferred looking at dusty old stuff in a museum!'

Bram led them onto Upper Guildford Street, past tall, elegant buildings with brightly painted doors, and then onto Russell Square. 'The Museum is just the other side of this park,' he said to Molly. 'We can stop in the park, if you like – I think Her Majesty might need a widdle?' Her Majesty *did* indeed need a widdle, and carried out that undertaking in the centre of a large, green lawn beside a small triangular hill of fresh soil. Looking around the park, Molly could see many little triangular hills, spread out all over the otherwise pristine lawn, looking as out-of-place as pimples on the face of the *Mona Lisa*.

'Mole hills,' said Bram, noting her puzzled expression. 'We don't have moles in Ireland – they're little furry fellows who burrow tunnels under the ground with big claws – but they have loads of 'em over here!' Her Majesty sniffed at the mole hill and looked up at Bram with what he thought may have been a disapproving expression – she obviously had little time for moles.

'Is there anywhere else that you're looking forward to seeing in London, Mol?' asked Bram, as they set off again. 'Do you have a list of places you simply *have* to visit?'

'The only place I'd really like to visit is Buckingham Palace where Queen Victoria lives.' She smiled a mischievous smile. 'I'm planning on bringing the dog along and seeing if I can introduce the real Her Majesty to Her Majesty, and if that doesn't work, I'll let her have another wee on the Queen's front lawn!'

Bram laughed; it was just like Molly to be disrespectful to Her Majesty Queen Victoria, ruler of

Great Britain and Ireland; that was why she had named her dog after her. Despite being Irish and therefore *technically* a subject of the Queen, Molly seemed to have as much time for old Queen Vic as Her Majesty had for moles.

They walked through the trees at the other side of the leafy square and down a pretty street full of high, redbrick houses with large doors built into white ground floors until they found themselves standing in front of the imposing entrance to the British Museum.

Molly gasped. The Museum was a grand building, much bigger than any building in Dublin. *It makes the General Post Office look like a doll's house,* she thought, marvelling at the rows of white columns that held up Museum's huge portico and its wings either side, *it even makes the Custom House look like a garden shed!* Molly thought that as grand as London seemed to be, from what she'd seen so far, she probably preferred Dublin – Dublin was just so much smaller and easier to get around. *Maybe it's because I'm a Dubliner, that I love Dublin Town …*

Flocks of pigeons flew overhead and landed to join their feathery brethren in the courtyard, where they became a moving carpet of grey and white plumage, filling up almost every inch. They flapped around, bumping into each other, pecking at invisible pieces of food on the flagstones and squabbling amongst themselves in shrill, COOing shrieks. At the far side of the courtyard was a set of wide stone steps that led up to a tall wooden door. With Her Majesty clearing a path through the panicking pigeons, Molly and Bram made their way towards the steps.

An old lady sat on the steps, wearing ragged clothes and a battered brown hat. She was surrounded by COOing pigeons and had a wicker basket full of small brown paper bags beside her. 'Feed the birds,' she called as she saw them approach. 'Oh, won't you feed the birds, young master and mistress? Fresh breadcrumbs, an' only a ha'penny a bag.' Bram fished in his pocket for a penny coin; he bought two bags of crumbs, and he and Molly threw the breadcrumbs onto the steps where they were instantly engulfed in a squawking swarm of feathers and beaks.

'C'mon,' said Molly shaking her head to dislodge one of the fluttering grey birds from her red curly hair, 'I like pigeons, but I don't want to be wearing one as a hat – let's go inside.'

Beyond the wooden door, the high-ceilinged lobby of the Museum was packed with people, but was, thankfully, pigeon-free. Molly and Bram were leading Her Majesty up to the cloakroom counter when a growing murmur swept over the crowd of Museum visitors as people started to whisper to each other, then to talk in louder voices that echoed off the lobby's alabaster pillars and high ceiling. A couple of people cried out in alarm and dismay, and one lady fainted into a heap onto the marble tiles

The crowd started to move as one out of the lobby and onto the steps outside as their voices rose. Puzzled, Bram and Molly followed them. On the steps of the Museum, groups of goggle-eyed people were crowded around, reading newspapers that were being sold by the armful by a shouting newspaper boy. Over the hubbub, Bram could make out some of the words the boy was calling out: 'Author' was one. 'World Famous' were two more. 'Missing' was another.

The breadcrumb seller was still sitting on her step beside her wicker basket, her pigeons frightened away by all the activity. The old lady's head was in her hands and an open newspaper lay on her lap.

'I say,' said Bram, 'do you by any chance know what is going on?'

She looked up at Molly and Bram, her eyes brimming with tears. 'It's Charles Dickens,' she said with a sob, 'our own dear Charlie.' Bram instinctively clutched at the jacket pocket that held his precious copy of *A Christmas Carol*. 'He's …' the pigeon lady wailed, holding up the front cover of the newspaper, 'He's … Oh lordy, young master … the great Charles Dickens is MISSING!'

NOTICE:

○

DICKENS MISSING

○

WITH A HEAVY HEART WE MUST ANNOUNCE THAT THE WORLD-FAMOUS, RENOWNED AUTHOR

MR CHARLES DICKENS IS MISSING

○

THE MUCH-ADMIRED MR DICKENS WAS LAST SEEN ON STAGE
AT THE LYCEUM THEATRE ON WELLINGTON STREET
ON THE EVENING OF FRIDAY THE TWENTY-FOURTH OF JULY
FOLLOWING A SUCCESSFUL SPEAKING ENGAGEMENT
AT THAT VENUE.

○

HIS LOVING AND DEVOTED FAMILY ARE OFFERING A

SUBSTANTIAL REWARD FOR

ANY INFORMATION WHICH MAY LEAD TO
MR DICKENS' SAFE RETURN.

○

MAKE HASTE TO APPLY TO THE DICKENS FAMILY
AT GAD'S HILL PLACE, HIGHAM, KENT OR TO HIS SON,
MASTER HENRY DICKENS, CURRENTLY LODGING AT
FORTY-EIGHT DOUGHTY STREET, LONDON

GOD SAVE THE QUEEN!

Chapter Five:

Stick 'Em Up, Monk, We're The Pun Lovin' Criminals

In which Billy the Pan has a difficult first day on the job

'That was a complete and utter disaster!' said Hetty angrily as the Sackville Street Spooks trudged dejectedly back through the hall door and into Madame Flo's front parlour. 'Billy's first time in charge of a bobbing caper and he makes an absolute *hames* of it!'

'Woah, lil' lady,' said Wild Bert. 'Why don't y'all grab yourselves a pew here on this here sofa and tell me what in the *Dickens* went down?'

Bert was a Wild West rodeo trick-rider, the self-proclaimed fastest six-gun this side of the Mississippi, and, most importantly, Madame Flo's husband. Since the Spooks' own home shack on the Royal Canal at the edge of Mud Island had been burned down by the Peelers, they had mostly been staying with Bert and Flo, and Bert and Flo, having no children themselves, were very happy to have them. As small as Madame Flo's little redbrick house at the side of Smithfield Square was, it was nice for the couple to have the excitement and bustle of young people around their home. The Spooks, in turn, did jobs for Bert and Flo – fetching groceries from the shops (paid for with actual money, a novelty for the Spooks, who were much more used to availing of their customary 'five-fingered discount'), cleaning and dusting, and using their knack of being able to acquire unusual items such as a live jellyfish, an authentic pirate flag, or sometimes even a stuffed Sumatran lesser-spotted mongoose, at short notice. The smallest of the Spooks, Calico Tom, practically worked full-time for Madame Flo as a teacup rattler in her fortune-telling business. It was little Tom's job to sit hidden under the round table where Flo sat to tell fortunes, and to make the teacup on the velvet tablecloth clatter around in its saucer while the Amazing and Uncanny Madame Florence – also known as the Seer of the What-Is-To-Come, the One Who Knows All, the Seventh Daughter of a Seventh Daughter, and the White Witch of Westmoreland Street – waved her ring-festooned fingers over a crystal ball while the gullible eejit at the other side of the table sat goggle-eyed with astonishment and fear.

Madame Flo, living up to her reputation as a fortune-telling clairvoyant, entered the room right on cue, ducking low so the tall ostrich feather on her purple turban would fit under the door frame, and carrying a large tray filled with biscuits and a big pot of steaming tea.

Although looking decidedly dejected, the Spooks dived on the tray and began to devour the biscuits.

'Ah, it wasn't really Billy's fault,' said Rose, through a mouthful of crumbs as Billy sat shamefaced and isolated on a threadbare armchair.

'Of *course* it was Billy's fault,' said Hetty, 'the lanky gob-daw.' Taking another biscuit from the tray, she turned to Wild Bert. 'It was the *Blind-Man's-Buff* caper,' she said, biting into her biscuit, 'where we block the light comin' into an alleyway so the Quality can't see where they're goin'.'

'And then you lot come out of the shadows like unseen ghosts and pick their pockets,' said Flo as she sat on the arm of Billy's chair.

'We're not called the Spooks for nothin',' said Rose, slurping from her teacup and reaching for a third biscuit.

'Well, this eejit,' Hetty jerked a thumb at Billy, 'chose that little laneway between Dame Street and Dame Lane; you know, the one that comes out at the Albion Hotel.'

'A good choice,' said Wild Bert, 'it's enclosed overhead like a tunnel – you could put bins either end and it would almost be as dark in there as a moonless night on the prairie.' He threw his head back and made a wolf-like AARRROOOOOO! sound.

Hetty shook her head and continued on. 'That's what we did,' she said, 'and then we hid and waited for some rich people to walk through who might like to make an anonymous contribution to the Keep-The-Sackville-Street-Spooks-Fed fund – pound notes, silk handkerchiefs, pocketbooks, that kind of stuff.' Flo nodded; everybody has to find their own way of making a living, and wasn't telling bogus, made-up fortunes to well-off dimwits with too much money practically the same thing as picking their pockets?

'After a few minutes, Billy tells us to watch out, that a big group of swells is on the way down the alley, headin' towards the Albion. We were rubbin' our hands together – if we could swindle a big load of rich eejits all together, we'd make enough money in one go to be able to take the rest of the day off!' She shot a poisonous look at Billy. 'So down the lane they come in the pitch dark, but when we try to pick-pocket them we find out that they've no pockets, and even if they did have pockets, they wouldn't have any money inside them – they weren't Quality at all, they were a group of Carmelite monks from Whitefriars Church! Monks wear long, *pocket-less* habits and have taken a vow of poverty; they were even more penniless than we were!'

'Heee-eey, you know, I wanted to be a monk once,' said Bert with a sly smile, 'but I just never got the chants. The *chants*!'

Rose groaned.

'And then,' continued Hetty, ignoring Bert's (admittedly weak) effort at humour, 'because Billy had forgotten to make one of us a lookout, who comes up the alley next but a couple of Peelers – they copped what we were up to, and they grabbed Shep before we could all get away! Poor Shep is stuck in a cell now in the police station at College Green!'

They all sat back while Hetty glared at Billy the Pan. Billy kept his eyes on the floor.

Wild Bert stroked his silver moustache and goatee beard thoughtfully and adjusted the snow-white Stetson on his head. 'It's times like these,' he said slowly in his Wild West cowboy drawl, 'that we have to think about W.W.M.D.'

'W.W.M.D.?' asked Rose. 'What's W.W.M.D., Bert?'

'What Would Molly Do?' Bert smiled.

Calico Tom raised a tiny hand and growled, 'Molly would march straight down to the station and break Shep out!' For such a small, baby-faced boy he had a deceptively deep voice.

'Well then, there's your answer!' said Wild Bert, standing up. 'We march down to the station, just like Molly would, and find a way a' breakin' li'l Shep outta the clink! There's gonna be a jailbreak! Can I get a YEE-HAW?'

The rest of the Spooks, including Billy, stood up and gave a quiet, unconvincing, 'Yee-haw …' in return.

Just then the parlour door swung open and, to their surprise, in came Shep, a huge smile on his face.

'Shep!' cried Billy the Pan with relief in his voice, delighted to see his pal. 'You got out all by yourself!'

Shep wiped his dribbling nose in his sleeve. 'Molly taught me a thing or two about pickin' locks, I had it open in a jiffy,' he said, helping himself to the last two remaining biscuits. 'And, sure, it was no bother to get out anyway; I didn't even have to sneak past the sergeant's desk – there was nobody there!'

'All the Peelers had been called out of the station; it was the same all over Dublin,' said Shep, 'every single police barracks is empty!' The boy started giggling, his face creasing up in almost uncontrollable mirth. 'There was a jailbreak tonight,' he said, his shoulders shaking, 'from Dublin Zoo! Loads of animals escaped – penguins, wolves, leopards, the giraffe, even a lion – an' all the Peelers have been dispatched to round 'em all up!'

CHAPTER SIX:

THERE'S NO BUSINESS LIKE SHOW BUSINESS

IN WHICH MOLLY AND BRAM MEET A YOUNG MAGICIAN AND
FIND A FEATHERY CLUE

Using Bram's map, Molly and Bram made their way down Museum Street and followed Drury Lane towards the River Thames. 'The Lyceum Theatre is on Wellington Street,' said Molly, reading the crumpled DICKENS MISSING notice as she walked along with Her Majesty's lead in her other hand. 'If there's a clue to where your old friend Charlie is, it will be there.'

'I wouldn't describe Mr Dickens as an *old friend*,' said Bram. 'We only met him that one time in the Rotunda Round Room – he's as much your friend as he is mine.'

'Ah, yeah,' said Molly, 'but *I'm* not his pen pal; old Charlie D. and *me* never exchanged letters like you two do.'

It was true that Bram and Charles Dickens, the world famous author, had exchanged letters, but the vast majority of the letter writing in the 'pen pal' relationship had been carried out by Bram – the boy had written numerous enthusiastic communications in which he profusely thanked the great author for his generous gift of the signed copy of *A Christmas Carol*, showered the great author with fulsome praise for his other works, and asked countless questions about the plots, characters and details of his many books from *Oliver Twist* to *The Old Curiosity Shop*, and from *Martin Chuzzlewit* to *David Copper-*

field. Each letter he had written neatly in black ink, sealed carefully with wax, and addressed accurately to Charles Dickens' publisher in London. For Dickens' part in the pen pal arrangement, he had sent back the sum-total of one reply; a letter that Bram had opened feverishly when he saw it on the door-mat and had treasured ever since. He actually had the letter about his person at that very moment; it was in the inside pocket of his jacket, folded and tucked carefully between the pages of his signed copy of his Dickens book. Reminded of the letter by Molly's words, he stopped, took it out and quickly re-read it.

Thursday 17th of February 1859

Gad's Hill Place, Higham,

Kent

Dear Master Stoker

Many thanks for the many, many letters you have sent; I am accustomed to receiving as many as fifty or sixty letters per day from various correspondents, but it seems you are endeavouring to double that number with your own efforts!

While I am very gratified by your effusive praise for my humble books, I am afraid if I were to answer each and every one of your innumerable inquiries about the same, I should be sitting at my desk from now until Christmas! My publisher is expecting the next instalment of my latest part-work publication, which I have entitled 'A Tale of Two Cities', at the end of each month, and would be very cross with me indeed if I abandoned my writing duties in favour of satisfying the enquiring mind of a young gentleman from Dublin.

Come and see me in Gad's Hill, young man, should you ever be in the vicinity; I should very much like to meet you again someday, and to answer your copious questions in person.

I remain, faithfully yours,

Charles Dickens.

Even though Bram was twelve, he realised that Dickens had probably issued the invitation in the secure knowledge that Bram would be highly unlikely to ever 'be in the vicinity' of the small village of Higham in Kent, and therefore there would be little or no danger of Dickens' peace – and, more importantly, his flow of writing – being disturbed by the arrival at the Gad's Hill door of a diminutive-but-bookish Irish admirer. And although Bram sometimes had daydreamed about taking a train to Higham and visiting his favourite author while he was in London, he had no real intention of doing so – he would have been far too nervous. But Bram was still delighted and thrilled to receive such a letter from a writer he considered his hero. He was also touched that a man of Dickens' brilliance should be so *kind* as to reply to him – a boy from Dublin whom the great author had met only once, and only fleetingly. But then, Dickens had a reputation for being kind to all. Bram had never known his real uncles, all three of his father's brothers had died before he was born, but he thought if he were ever to have an uncle – a kindly, encouraging, *fun* uncle – Mr Charles Dickens would have been the prime candidate to fill that role. Bram sighed. *Good old Uncle Charlie!*

'That's it,' he said to Molly, in as steely and determined a voice as he could summon, 'we have to find out what happened to Charles Dickens; we simply *must* – and the best place to get on the trail of the missing author is to start right at the very start, as it were. The Lyceum Theatre is where he went missing from, so we need to get inside the theatre and see if we can find any clues as to where poor Uncle, I mean, *Mr* Dickens might be!'

'Well, Bram,' said Molly as they came out into Wellington Street, 'we may not be the only ones with that idea.'

The street was thronged with so many people that Molly and Bram could barely see the front of the Lyceum Theatre. The crowd was an odd mish-mash of young people, old people and people in the middle – the richest of the rich with their shiny top hats, silver canes, *pince-nez* spectacles and noses held aloft, and the very poorest of the poor with torn pinafores and dresses, tangled hair in need of a wash, and grubby bare feet. All of them, Bram realised, must be distressed Dickens fans; they must have all had the same idea that Molly and Bram had – to go to directly the last place Dickens had been seen. Some stood in solemn silence, with tears running down their cheeks, while others shouted their displeasure

and outrage at the great author's sudden disappearance, their faces red and angry. "Oo has taken Dickens?' they wailed. 'What shall I do for my next instalment of *Cities* – what is to 'appen to Jerry Cruncher?'
Bram knew that Dickens' latest book, *A Tale of Two
Cities,* was being serialised in a weekly magazine, it
had been since the April of that year and, like all
Dicken's part-work books, it was very popular. But,
unfortunately, and despite Bram's pleading, his father
didn't subscribe to *All the Year Round,* and Bram had
no idea who this Cruncher character was.

The mob were facing the doors of theatre, where a
dozen top-hatted, serious-looking policemen stood
guard in front of the six tall columns that held up
the portico, with their black truncheon day-sticks
in their hands. As the two friends, pulling a very
reluctant Her Majesty behind them, pushed their
way through the jostling crowd towards the theatre
entrance, Molly surveyed the twelve scowling burly
officers of the law.

She turned to Bram and shook her head. 'We'll
never get past these fellas,' she whispered. 'These
London police jokers are tougher than the eejits

we have in Dublin; they don't mess around – they'd wallop their own grannies with those truncheons just for lookin' crooked at them. There's no way we're gettin' into the theatre by the front door.' Being a part-time pickpocket, Molly knew the workings and methods of the police in her own hometown inside-out and made it her business to study the police services of other countries just in case she ever decided to carry out any pickpocketing pursuits while on a weekend break.

Bram nodded. 'We'll have to find another way in,' he whispered back. 'Maybe there's a stage door somewhere around the side?'

They pushed through the crowd to a small lane at the right of the theatre which, in contrast to Wellington Street with its multitude of angry and upset Londoners, was almost deserted. They found the theatre's stage door at the end of the lane; it was a heavy double door, wide enough to take in the big, painted flats that are used for onstage scenery and sets. Bram gave the door a push; it didn't budge. 'As I thought,' he said, 'locked.' Molly handed Bram Her Majesty's lead and bent down to the lock, taking her trusty ring of lock-picks from her ginger hair. As she started to stick the pick into the keyhole, the heavy doors swung outwards and a black shape flew out past Molly's head, as if it had been flung with great force. The shape landed on the cobblestones behind them with a thud.

'An' don't come back!' roared a voice from the doorway. A brawny woman stood glowering in the open door, her massive hands on her even bigger hips. 'If I catch you around 'ere again, *The Astounding 'arry Dee*,' she said, her voice dripping with sarcasm, 'I shall box your ears good an' prop-ah! You see if I don't!'

From his hiding place behind the door, Bram peeped up at the formidable, angry door keeper and her colossal, musclebound arms. *She must have gotten those big arms from taking in scenery*, he thought, *and throwing it out. Even if Molly can pick the lock, we'll never get past that humungous harridan!*

The doors slammed and Molly and Bram, their eyebrows raised almost to their hairlines, looked around into the street to see whom, or what, the large woman had so violently deposited onto the cobblestones. The shape in the centre of the laneway slowly stood up and began to brush the dust from his long-tailed black suit jacket and grey trousers. He was a tallish chap, a good two inches taller than Bram, but when he pushed back the brim of his battered top hat from his face, Molly and Bram could see that he was a boy of around their age. His eyes were bright blue and friendly, if a little sad, and his face was covered in freckles. 'I say,' he said, his accent quite cultured and mild, and certainly not as rough and fierce as the voice of the woman who had thrown him out of the theatre, 'you chaps didn't happen to notice where my magic wand went, did you?'

'Your ...' asked Bram, a puzzled look on his face, '... magic wand?'

'Black in the middle,' said the boy, his eyes scanning the gutters at either side of the lane, 'white at each end; I think it may have flown out my pocket whilst I was flying out of the door.'

'Is this what you're lookin' for?' asked Molly, holding up a black wooden rod by its white-painted end. 'It is!' cried the boy, 'but don't press on that white end too hard!'

'Like this?' said Molly, and squeezed the end; to Bram's surprise, a bunch of fake, feathery flowers exploded out of the end with a quiet POPP. The boy clapped his hands together and waggled his fingers with a flourish and a loud 'Ta-DAAAA!' Her Majesty barked a WOOF and grinned a doggy smile.

Molly cocked an unimpressed eye at the grinning boy and tossed the flower-topped magic wand in his direction. He caught it, but immediately fumbled and dropped it. 'Think that's the first time I've seen a magic trick?' said Molly. 'Some of my best friends are magicians.'

'ARE they?' said the boy, his eyes wide. 'I've always wanted to be a magician and to be on the stage. My father taught me loads of magic tricks – and he's always encouraging me to audition for shows. That's what I was trying to–'

Molly's face lit up and she quickly interrupted the boy. 'Maybe that's how we get past that gigantic battle-axe at the stage door,' she said excitedly to Bram, 'we pretend to be a couple of performing children, lookin' for our big break on the London stage!'

'I suppose,' said Bram slowly, 'that we could do that jokey music hall routine thing that we do sometimes in the evening in Madame Flo's to keep Rose and Shep entertained; but we'd have to rehearse it firs–'

But he, like the young magician before him, didn't get time to finish his sentence – Molly was already banging hard on the stage door with her fist.

The door opened and the huge woman stood before them. Out of the corner of his eye, Bram noticed the Astounding 'arry Dee, quickly take his topper off and slip behind them so he couldn't be seen.

'Hallooooo!' said Molly with a bright smile and the twinkliest tone she could muster. 'Thank you so much for seeing us!' She barged past the lady into the theatre.

Bram hastily handed Her Majesty's leash to the young would-be magician behind him. 'Watch my dog for me, won't you?' he hissed. The boy nodded, and Her Majesty licked his hand. Bram nodded his thanks back and followed Molly into the theatre backstage area. Her Majesty would be safe enough in the care of 'arry Dee, he thought.

'Hey, 'old on one minute,' growled the large woman as Bram pulled the door closed behind them, sealing them in. ''Oo, do you two fink you are, ven?'

'We,' said Molly, standing with her arms outstretched and grinning a grin that showed almost all of her teeth, 'are here for our audition! We, good madam, are the world-famous child comedy duo, newly arrived from a sell-out, six-week, smash-hit tour of Dublin City, the hilarious, the hysterical, the– the–' She racked her brain for another word that started with H.

'Humorous?' suggested Bram.

'The *humorous* ...' continued Molly, 'MALONE & STOKER!'

'A-hem,' a-hemmed Bram, 'she means Stoker & Malone.'

The woman snorted and folded her thick arms, 'Never 'eard of ya.'

'Madam!' gasped Molly in mock outrage. 'You mean to say you've never heard of Malone & Stoker? Why, our *Daddy's Dead Duck* routine is the toast of Donnycarney, our *Bicycle Made for Three* song is sung all over Summerhill, and our *Are You My Egyptian Mummy?* sketch made several patrons in the Theatre Royal pee their pants!'

The woman opened her mouth to speak, but Molly quickly cut across her. 'Perhaps you'd like a demonstration,' she said, 'before we show our act to the manager? A private little performance to show you how good we are, and why we are the best and most side-splitting comical-kid double-act ever to come out of Ireland?'

The huge woman shrugged noncommittedly; Molly took this as a *yes* and winked at Bram. 'Follow my lead,' she hissed quietly.

At once, Molly began to march around in a circle, arching her elbows and pumping her fists rhythmically. Bram was unsure what she was up to, but did as he was told and followed her lead, marching in step behind her.

Molly came to a sudden stop and Bram banged into her back with a quiet *OW*. 'I say, I say, I say,' said Molly, her index finger up in the air, 'what do you call a boomerang that doesn't come back?'

'I don't know,' said Bram, beginning to get the idea, 'what *do* you call a boomerang that doesn't come back?'

'A stick!' said Molly, and stared marching again, this time humming a tune as she went. Bram joined in with the humming and the marching, but only managed to march for five steps before he banged into Molly's back again. The large woman was still scowling at them, although Bram thought her eyes looked less narrow and marginally less murderous than before.

'I say, I say, I say,' said Molly, 'why was the actor sent to jail?'

'I don't know,' said Bram, 'why *was* the actor sent to jail?'

Molly clapped her hands together and wiggled her fingers in the same way she had seen the Astounding 'arry Dee do moments before, 'Because he was caught *stealing* the show!'

They started marching and humming again. Then woman's scowling mouth began to twitch at the edges.

Molly stopped again; this time Bram skidded to a halt and just avoided crashing into her back.

'I say, I say, I say,' said Molly, grinning, 'why is Queen Victoria like a big baker's shop?'

'I don't know,' said Bram, 'why *is* Queen Victoria like a big baker's shop?'

'Because,' said Molly, 'they both have massive bloomers!'

The huge woman's face began to tremble, and her shoulders started to shake. She threw her head back and laughed a series of loud, braying, honking laughs. 'Aw-right, aw-right,' she said, wiping her eyes, 'you can go and see the manager; Mr Taylor should be taking tea in 'is office on the other side of the stage – you tell 'im Edna said for you to visit 'im.'

'Thanks so much, Edna,' chirped Molly, and the two friends trotted off down the dark corridor that led to the stage.

Before they walked out onto the wooden boards of the Lyceum stage, Molly peeped around the curtains into the auditorium. 'Peelers!' she whispered back to Bram. 'They must be lookin' for clues!' Bram chanced a look around the curtain. The auditorium was cavernous, and its tall walls were decorated with expensive-looking flock wallpaper and draped with plush red velvet curtains. Walking slowly between the rows of plump, comfortable seats were at least twenty navy-uniformed policemen. The Peelers were stopping every now and then as they walked, bending as if to inspect something on the floor. *Hah*, thought Bram, *it's almost like they think Mr Dickens might have been hidden away under a seat all along!* He glanced up to the ornate, gold-painted balcony; more police constables, their long moustaches twitching with concentration, were walking back and forth up there too.

Molly tapped him on the shoulder. 'Quality,' she whispered, 'we'll never be able to have a good look at the stage with all those Bobbies lumbering about, but I have a plan – I'm going to ask you a question, and whatever I ask you, you just shout *Right-ho!* Alright?'

Bram nodded; he had no idea what Molly had planned, but knew from experience that her plans, even her most outlandish and wacky ones, usually worked out. *Usually*.

'OI!' she shouted loudly from behind the curtain in a vague approximation of a London accent, 'Stage Manage-ah! Pull the curtain like a good chap, won't-cha?'

'RIGHT-HO!' shouted Bram, and Molly started to pull the stage curtains across, hauling down on the ropes at the side of the stage arm over arm until the curtains swished closed. The policemen in the auditorium looked up briefly at the curtains as they drew together concealing the stage, and then went back about their work. They had their job, to investigate a great author's disappearance, and, they supposed, the Stage Manager of the Lyceum Theatre must have *his* job to do too.

'Alone at last!' said Molly as they walked out onto the stage. Dickens' wooden reading lectern stood alone at the centre of the stage, the very same one the world-renowned novelist had used for his dramatic reading of *A Christmas Carol* in the Dublin's Rotunda Round Room the year before – the lectern that held his sleeping cap, his candle, his ink and quill pen, and the copy of the book that he sometimes held, but seldom referred to, as he did his reading. Bram and Molly had been present for that event in the Round Room, sneaking into the sold-out performance by slipping through a second-floor window at the venue and sitting unseen at the side of the stage. Bram had been awestruck by Dickens' reading; the great author had put on an astonishing show, pacing the stage and waving his arms, inhabiting every character from the book as he performed.

One moment he was bent over, crackly-voiced and twisted, as he played the miserable miser Ebeneezer Scrooge; the next he was cheery and chipper as he played Scrooge's kind-hearted nephew Fred; but it was Dickens' creepy and sinister portrayal of Marley's ghost that had sent shivers down both Bram and Molly's spines. Bram had always adored reading the books, but seeing the great man bring his own book to life had cemented Dickens' place in Bram's heart as the boy's favourite author.

After the reading, Dickens had gifted Bram the copy of *A Christmas Carol* that he had been reading from, signing his autograph on the title page with his long white feather quill pen. Bram still carried the book with him in his jacket pocket wherever he went. Bram walked straight to the lectern and couldn't resist running his fingers over its velvet-covered top. *We have to find him!*

'Right. What are we looking for?' asked Molly, already on her hands and knees, peering at the wooden boards of the stage floor.

'I'm not entirely sure,' said Bram. 'Anything that might give us a clue as to what happened to poor Mr

Dickens.' The wooden floor was dusty and scuffed here and there from the thousands of actors who had trodden the boards in the thirty or so years since the theatre had opened. Apart from the chest-high lectern, the only other furniture on the stage was a chair that was lying on its side. 'It looks like he might have been grabbed,' said Bram, standing back with his hands on his hips, taking in the view of the whole stage. 'This chair looks like it might have been knocked over in some sort of scuffle.'

'Hold on,' said Molly, still on her hands and knees, 'I think I might have found something!' she fished around in her curly bush of ginger hair for her lock-picking tools and ran the selection of thin metal implements through her fingers until she found what she was looking for – a skinny tool that resembled a tweezers.

Bram joined her on the floor. 'Mol,' he said, 'this is no time to pluck your eyebrows!' Molly stuck out her tongue at him and bent back to the floorboards, inserting the tweezers tool into the crack between two of them. 'I'm not trying to pluck my eyebrows,' she said, her face creased in concentration, 'I'm just wondering who thought that the stage of the

Lyceum was a good place to pluck a chicken!' She carefully drew out the tweezers from the crack; in between the prongs was a small, bright green feather. Molly held it up to Bram. 'I've never heard of a *green* chicken,' he said. 'Maybe it's a London breed of bird.'

There was a sound of footsteps from the side of the stage. 'The Peelers!' hissed Molly. 'They're coming up the steps onto the stage!'

'Time for us to take our bow and exit, stage right,' whispered Bram. He stuck the green feather into his jacket pocket, and they swiftly and silently slid into the wings at the opposite side.

The two friends tiptoed past a closer door marked THEATRE MANAGER and quietly crept down the dark corridor at the back of the stage, emerging in the hallway at the stage door. Edna, the large stage-door custodian, was sitting on a tiny stool, drinking tea from a tiny bone China teacup with her chunky little finger daintily raised up. 'Well,' she growled, 'ow did you get on wiv Mr Taylor?'

Bram looked blankly back at her.

'The audition,' whispered Molly, 'with the theatre manager.'

'Oh,' said Bram, 'he said if belly laughs were penny coins, we'd be two bob short of a tanner. I'm not quite sure what that means, but I think he liked us.' They gave Edna a quick wave and walked out through the stage door.

At the far side of the narrow street the Astounding 'arry Dee leapt to his feet, adjusting the battered topper on his head. He trotted across to them with a very delighted dog beside him. Molly hugged Her Majesty and her faithful canine companion licked her face in return.

'Thanks for looking after our dog for us, 'arry,' said Bram, taking the end of the leash back from the young magician's hand.

'Did you find any clues?' asked 'arry eagerly.

'Clues?' said Molly, removing her face from Her Majesty's sloppy but affectionate attention and standing up. 'What do you mean, *clues*? Hold on, are *you* on the trail of old Charlie Dickens too?'

The boy took off his top hat and wrung the brim between his hands. 'Yes,' he said, 'I *am* on the trail of Charles Dickens, as it happens.' He popped the topper back on his head and tapped it with his magic

NOTICE:

HAVE YOU SEEN CHARLES DICKENS?

THE MOST VENERABLE AUTHOR, MR

CHARLES DICKENS IS MISSING

HIS LOVING FAMILY ARE OFFERING A

SUBSTANTIAL REWARD

FOR ANY INFORMATION ON MR DICKENS' WHEREABOUTS

PLEASE MAKE PROMPT CONTACT WITH THE DICKENS FAMILY
AT GAD'S HILL PLACE, HIGHAM, KENT OR TO HIS
LOVING SON, MASTER HENRY DICKENS, CURRENTLY AT
FORTY-EIGHT DOUGHTY STREET, LONDON

MAKE HASTE AND GOD SAVE THE QUEEN!

wand; the bunch of feathery flowers POPPed back out of the end and he pushed it back in mild embarrassment. 'You see,' said the Astounding 'arry Dee, 'Charles Dickens ... is my father!'

CHAPTER SEVEN:

SMITHFIELD GOES APE!

IN WHICH BILLY THE PAN VISITS THE FAIR AND FINDS SOMETHING FOUL

Billy the Pan sat up and stretched. Although he had his own family home in Gloucester Street, a tenement room he shared with his ma, his da, and a great number of brothers and sisters, he much preferred to stay here in Madame Flo's house with the rest of the Sackville Street Spooks. In Gloucester

Street he had to share a bed with four brothers, all of whom were getting bigger and sharper-elbowed every day. Here in Flo's, Billy had a rug on the parlour floor completely to himself, and, even better, his best friend Shep slept across the room on another rug just like his. He looked over to Shep's rug; he could see his blanket and his blue ticking stripe pillow, but there was no sign of Shep. Billy remembered that Smithfield Fair was on that morning, and he knew that Shep always liked to get down to the market early. The smaller boy loved to play with the baby sheep, goats and piglets before they were sold by the farmers who brought them, and the carnival folk let him have goes on the merry-go-round and the swing-boats for free before the crowds built up.

Billy stood and was reaching for the battered pan he always wore on his head when the parlour door opened.

'C'mon, Billy, gerrup!' said Rose, smiling. 'Flo said she left you some toast in the kitchen – you don't want to be late for the carnival!'

Holding a piece of buttered toast between his teeth like a dog, Billy trotted the short distance to

Smithfield Square with Rose. As usual on fair day, the Square was jam-packed with sheep, pigs, chickens and cows, as well as horses, ponies, donkeys, goats and geese, all fenced into small pens that almost completely covered the cobblestones. Any other space was taken up by a multitude of people who were smiling and laughing as they chatted with friends and surveyed the animals. Billy loved the sound of this chatter, mixed with the whinnies, baas, neighs and oinks of the animals, but most of all he loved the wheezing music of the carnival calliope, the steam-driven pipe organ played on the back of a brightly-painted wagon by a uniformed musician. Its cheerful notes bounced off the walls of the Square and never failed to put a little joy into people's hearts.

After the disastrous caper with the Capuchin monks the night before, Billy was glad that today was fair day – the Spooks, as a rule, never worked when the fair was on. The only member of the gang who did was Calico Tom who, Billy imagined, was probably busy hiding under the velvet-covered crystal ball table in Madame Florence's carnival tent, rattling teacups as he helped her gently swindle pennies from naïve eejits as they got their fortunes told.

Billy sat down on a haybale beside a pen where two fine chestnut stallions stood clacking their teeth and stamping their hooves on the straw-covered cobbles. While he finished his toast, a couple of older men wearing shabby work clothes and threadbare hats greeted him and Rose, then rapped on Billy's hat for luck and passed him a ha'penny or two. Billy smiled to himself and closed his eyes in the morning sunshine, the embarrassment of the debacle the night before almost fading from his mind.

All at once the horses in the pen beside Billy and Rose became agitated, snorting loudly, stamping their hooves hard and blowing out air force-fully through their nostrils. There was a single far-off cry from somewhere in the crowd of people, which was followed almost immediately by a great, collective noise – almost a groan – that started low and then grew in intensity as more and more people joined in.

People close to Billy and Rose looked around, all of a sudden wary, their eyes wide with the promise of panic. Then one voice rose above the hubbub, a shrill voice that shouted one clear word: 'MONSTER!'

There was the sound of tearing cloth, like a ship's sail being rendered by a lightning-struck mast, followed by a crash of broken glass and then another cry of 'MONSTER!' The cry was taken up by the crowd, 'MONSTER!' and then it seemed to Billy that the crowd began to move as one, away from the south end of the Square, their pace growing quicker as they scrambled. The two stallions were jittering in their pen, the larger one rearing up in fright.

Suddenly a familiar face appeared from the throng. 'Shep!' shouted Billy the Pan, as he held onto Rose's hand to prevent her being swept away with the crowd. 'What's going on?'

'Billy!' said Shep. 'You've got to come to the side-show tents! There's something down there; something HUGE!' He looked behind him in fear and then back to Billy and Rose. 'It got into the tent – I think it's got Calico and Flo!'

With Shep and Rose following behind him, Billy made his way through the now thinning crowd towards the carnival ride and tents at the Liffey end of the Square. They passed abandoned enclosures and pens holding forsaken animals, all of whom were huddled into the pen corners, confused and frightened by the tumult. The fenced-off gate to the carnival had been abandoned too, and the painted laughing clowns' faces, fluttering butterflies and trumpeting elephants on the carnival signage looked somehow forbidding instead of welcoming. The calliope music had stopped, the organ player having deserted his post and run away.

A short distance away, Billy could see that the neat row of sideshow tents, erected every week for the different carnival acts, was partially in ruins; three of the tents had been ripped apart, their canvas walls torn and scattered and their fabric roofs flattened. A small crowd stood staring at one structure that was still standing, their hands up to their faces in shock. Loud, animal, guttural grunts and the sound of smashing wood and tearing fabric were coming from inside the multicoloured canvas walls of the tent; walls that Billy, to his dismay, recognised.

'Flo!' he shouted. 'Calico!' He ran towards the entrance flap, but Hetty, detaching herself from the small, horror-stricken crowd of onlookers, held him back.

There was a ripping sound as whatever was inside the tent began to tear its way out again through the canvas wall. The multicoloured fabric bulged, then split down the seam as two, mighty, hairy hands pulled it apart, revealing the furious face of a huge, black-furred creature. The monster stared at the crowd with dark eyes, sparkling with intelligence, and bared its snow-white teeth in a terrifying snarl. Lifting its long, muscular arms, it beat on its chest like a jungle drum, then it shuffled forward on two stocky but powerful legs and roared a ROAW-WRRRRRR so loud and deep that the children could feel their own ribs vibrate.

'Billy,' said Shep in a small voice as Rose clutched at his arm, 'I th-think that's o-one of the things the p-p-Peelers are lookin' for, that escaped from the zoo.'

'Oh, my holy mammy,' said Hetty, her voice shaking, 'it's … it's a GORILLA!'

CHAPTER EIGHT

YE OLDE CHESHIRE CHEESE

IN WHICH MOLLY AND BRAM MEET A BIG CHEESE, VISIT AN OLD
CHEESE, AND RUFFLE SOME FEATHERS

Bram stepped back in astonishment and gaped at Molly; it seemed the Astounding Harry Dee, despite his ineptitude at performing magic tricks, actually had the power to astound after all!

'So, the Dee stands for Dickens!' said Bram.

The would-be magician nodded. 'Harry Dickens at your service,' he said, taking off his topper and giving a deep bow. 'Well, *Henry* Dickens really, but my father calls me Harry.'

'I was at our lodgings when the maid woke me to tell me Papa was missing,' he continued. 'We stay up in London, you see, when Father has business or speaking engagements; we lodge at Doughty Street, in the very house that Father used to live in before I was born. He loves it there, it's so warm and cosy; he calls it his little haystack in the city. He says he and I are just like two little mice there, snuggling away in the straw.' The boy sighed. 'I used to prefer it to our house in the country, but after this, I'm not too sure.'

'Is that Gad's Hill Place?' asked Bram. 'Your father wrote to me and told me to visit him there!'

'Oh,' said Harry, 'Papa gives that invitation to an awful lot of people – he's so good-natured and he writes so many letters, you see; he just can't stop writing – and every other day we get a knock on the door from someone Father has asked to come to Gad's Hill. "Come and see me," he'll say, and what do you know, they *do* – by the bucketload!'

Bram thought about the letter tucked inside his copy of *A Christmas Carol* and was secretly very glad he hadn't taken up the offer to visit.

'I got word from Gad's Hill that Ellen and my sisters had engaged the services of a couple of detectives to help find Dad,' said Harry, rolling his eyes, 'but I am familiar with their work – Father used the same gentlemen before on another matter, and in my opinion they are a pair of absolute bumbling idiots – so I thought I'd better come down to the Lyceum and see if I could spot anything for myself. I cadged my way past the constables at the front door and was on my way to the stage when old Edna snared me like a white rabbit in a top hat.' He tapped his topper with his wand. The bunch of flowers exploded out of the wand again with a POPP. He sighed again, 'I suppose she's seen me audition too many times; I don't think she likes my magic act. Besides that, she only knows me by my stage name, the Astounding Harry Dee – she doesn't know that my father is Charles Dickens himself!'

'We managed to get onto the stage,' said Molly, 'and we think we might have found somethin'.'

Bram fished in his pocket and brought out the green feather they had discovered between the cracks in the stage floor woodwork; he held it up in the morning sunlight that streamed into the laneway.

'It's not a quill feather,' said Bram. 'Your father's quill pen is white.'

Harry took the feather in his fingers and furrowed his eyebrows. 'Hmmm,' he said, 'I don't …' His eyebrows shot up and he took off his top hat. 'MYRTLE!' he exclaimed. 'This simply *must* belong to Myrtle!'

'Who is Myrtle?' asked Molly. 'Is she a writer friend of your father's? Oh! Does she wear a fancy green feather boa that this feather fell off?'

'Myrtle doesn't *wear* feathers,' said Harry, 'she's *covered* in 'em!' Molly and Bram looked at each other in bewilderment. 'Myrtle is a *parrot*!' grinned Harry. 'And not just any old parrot, she's the rudest parrot in all of London!' The boy raised his arms and flapped them like a bird. 'She lives in a tavern and flies all around over peoples' heads screeching out the most horrendous insults! She's always calling people *ratbags* or *hornswogglers* – she once called a baldy vicar a *fly rink*, and even called my poor father a *dimber-damber*!'

Molly and Bram exchanged another bemused look; they didn't have these London insults back in Dublin, and neither of the friends knew what any of them actually meant.

'Father goes to the tavern to write sometimes; he says that Myrtle swooping over the customers' heads and screeching bad words at them inspires him,' said Harry with a proud smile. 'Myrtle repeats bits of peoples' conversations too, and don't tell anyone this,' the young magician looked around conspiratorially, 'but Father writes down anything funny the parrot says and uses it in his books! He hasn't been there since our last visit to London, though, and that was five weeks ago, as far as I know. That green feather definitely didn't fall from Father's clothes ...'

'Where is this tavern?' asked Bram. 'Is it far? It sounds like it may be a promising place to take up the trail.'

The boy shook his head. 'It's not far; it's in Fleet Street,' he said, popping his topper back on, 'not more than fifteen minutes' walk from here. It's called

Ye Olde Cheshire Cheese. The tavern is a bit of a rough joint – there are always loads of hooligans and rowdy ruffians frequenting the place. That's why Father likes it so much; he loves to be amongst the real, salt-of-the-earth London folk.' The boy grinned again, 'The ruffians are the ones who taught Myrtle all the bad words!'

'Well, 'arry Dee,' said Molly, 'I'm Molly and this is Bram.' She bent down to the dog who was busy licking Harry's hand. 'You've already met Her Majesty,' she smiled, 'We are going to help you find your father!'

* * *

They walked up the Strand, a street of fine, tall, white-stone buildings, past the little Church of St Clement Danes that stood incongruously in the centre of the road, with horse-drawn traffic bustling by ('That was designed and built by Sir Christopher Wren,' said Bram, while Molly inwardly expressed an opinion that Bram should not read so much), and then onto Fleet Street. In the distance the children could see the green dome of St Paul's Cathedral.

'Another one built by our ol' pal Chris Wren,' said Molly before Bram could say a word.

'Fleet Street is named for the River Fleet, that now flows underground – underneath the street,' said Bram, only slightly miffed that Molly had stolen his thunder in front of their new friend. 'It's now known,' he said to Harry, 'as the centre of newspaper and periodical publishing in the world.'

'I know,' said Harry. 'My father has published stories and books with most of the publishers here!'

The street was busy, with street sellers noisily calling out their wares for sale in sing-song voices and crowds of people swarming the sidewalks. The middle of the street was dug up in places, and many carriage drivers were loudly voicing their displeasure at the hold ups, while their horses stamped their hooves on the cobblestones and panted in the summer heat.

'They are trying to dig a tunnel for one of the new underground railway lines they are planning,' said Harry, 'but I think they forgot about the Fleet River – their tunnel keeps on filling up with water!'

Underground trains, thought Bram, *what a wonderfully eccentric idea!*

The tavern they were looking for faced onto the street – Molly spotted the swinging sign for *Ye Old Cheshire Cheese* as it creaked back and forth in the light morning breeze, its neglected fixings clearly in need of a good oiling – an entrance to the inn was to the left of the sign, down a dark, enclosed lane.

'Be careful, Bram,' said Molly, grabbing Bram's arm before they entered the murky passageway, 'this area isn't the most high-falutin and this laneway is perfect for a spot of *Blind-Man's-Buff*!'

Blind-Man's-Buff? thought Bram. *We're on the trail of the great Charles Dickens, we don't have time for parlour games!*

As it happened, Molly didn't need to be worried that a gang of ne'er-do-wells was about to assail them in the pitch-dark alleyway with the tried-and-trusted *Blind-Man's-Buff* caper – there were *already* a couple of people in the alley being assailed by a gang of ne'er-do-wells.

A group of three young lads, no older than ten, and a brown-haired girl of around nine were stalking in circles around two small, bowler-hatted gentlemen, making COOO-ing, pigeon-like noises to bamboo-

127

zle them, and reaching out their grubby hands in the dark, patting the pockets of the unfortunate men's black jackets and grey, stripey trousers, looking for gold watches, pocketbooks and silk handkerchiefs. The children were dressed in ragged clothes that made Molly think about the torn, faded blue dress and shabby pinafore that she used to wear, back in the days when she was a full-time pickpocket.

Bram made a move to rescue the two unlucky gentlemen, but Molly shook her head to stop him, motioned for him and Harry to be quiet, and then leaned back on the alleyway wall to admire the young gang's work.

The girl's technique was quite good, Molly thought – she was fast and slippery as an eel as she slid around, checking each of the two hapless gentlemen's pockets in turn. Two of the boys were reasonably gifted too, but the third boy, a very short lad with a red face, a barrel chest, slightly goggly, frog-like eyes and two thick eyebrows that meshed together at the top of his stubby nose, was the most talented of all, and to her surprise, Molly recognised the tiny chap as the same boy who she had seen performing the *Lost*

Baby caper so expertly at Westminster Bridge earlier that day. *This must be the same gang!*

The boy's tiny stature still reminded her of Calico Tom, but watching him work up close, Molly thought this small feller, unlike Calico, was a *born* pickpocket. He seemed to have an inbuilt ability to know which pocket held the greatest treasures and his fingers moved at lightning speed, dipping in and out of the gentlemen's jackets and removing fine silk handkerchiefs, pound notes and gold watches with immaculate ease.

'Alright,' said Molly eventually, pushing herself away from the wall, 'that's enough.' The four children stopped what they were doing and swivelled their heads around toward Molly, noticing her for the first time. They looked her, Bram and Harry up and down in an appraising manner. The smallest boy stood to his full, diminutive height and clicked his fingers. At once the two other boys reached up to the two gentlemen's heads and sharply pulled their bowler hats down over their eyes. The two men sat down heavily on the cobblestones of the alleyway, each grunting and straining as they tried to pull their hats up by the brims, but both hats seemed to be stuck fast onto their small heads.

'Oo' are you free, ven?' said one of the taller boys.

'Who we *free*, I mean we *three*, are is none of your business, young sir,' said Bram indignantly.

'Aye,' said the tiny boy, his eyebrow furrowing. 'Ah've seen ye before – I never forget a face – but I dinnae ken where.'

'Westminster Bridge, this morning,' said Molly,. 'You and your gang here were pulling a *Lost Baby* caper.' The small chap's eyebrow shot up; she knew about the *Lost Baby* caper?

'We,' said Molly grandly, 'are Malone, M. and Stoker, B., two verified members of the Sackville Street Spooks, street gang number 173, registered in Dublin with the Irish Brotherhood of Beggarmen.'

'And my name is Molly Malone,' continued Molly, 'apprentice level third grade with the Worshipful Company of Fishmongers, Hibernian Chapter, and widely acknowledged as the supreme sneak thief, the foremost fingersmith and most peerless pickpocket in all of Dublin City.' Molly then made a sign with her left hand, sticking out her thumb and bending in her index and middle fingers, and at the same time she brought the little finger of her right hand up to touch her nose. To Bram's surprise, the small boy with the unibrow made the exact same sign back to her. His demeanour, previously having been pugnacious, as if he had been ready for a fight, suddenly became more deferential.

'And I,' said Harry in a theatrical voice, 'am the Astounding Harry Dee! ALA-KA-BASHH!' With a dramatic flourish he threw three small paper wraps onto the ground. They made three tiny, barely audible PUTTing sounds when they hit the cobblestones, and a miniature wisp of smoke escaped from the top of each. 'I am so sorry,' he apologised meekly, 'I'm still working on the correct formula for my smoke bombs.'

The small boy made a snorting noise and ignored Harry. 'Aye,' he said in a thick Scottish accent. 'Ah'm a part-time fishmonger too. They call me Shetland Tony, on account of the fact that I'm from bonny Scotland.'

'Oh,' said one of the other boys, 'I fought you wuz called vat becoz you wuz small an' tiny, like a Shetland pon—'

'Don't say that!' neighed Shetland Tony. 'Ah'm called Shetland Tony because Ah'm Scottish an' ma name is Tony!' The other boy backed away. Shetland Tony may have been small, but he certainly commanded respect.

'Oor gang is called the Long Acre Lads,' said Tony.

'And Lassies!' said the girl.

'And Lassies,' agreed Tony with a short, equine sigh. 'Ah wasn't told that there was to be any other gangs working the Fleet Street patch today?'

'Don't worry,' said Molly, 'we're not lookin' for work; we're on our holidays.'

'We're actually looking for someone,' said Bram, 'maybe you could help us.'

'It's Charles Dickens!' blurted Harry, 'He's my Fa—'

Molly slapped her hand around Harry's mouth. 'What Harry wants to say,' she said, 'is that ol' Charlie Dickens is his favourite author.'

'Well 'e's everyone's favourite aww-fer, inny?' said one of the taller boys. 'Eliza 'ere loves 'im, duntcha, Eliza?' The small girl pickpocket wiped her nose with her sleeve and nodded enthusiastically.

'Aye,' said Shetland Tony, 'we heard he's gone missing; the word on the cobbles is that he's been kidnapped. An' you're spendin' your holidays lookin' for him?' Molly nodded.

'Right enough,' said Tony, 'I s'pose ye might as well, lassie – London's a bit rubbish, if you ask me.'

'Oi!' said one of the taller boys, but as quietly as he could.

'We have'nae seen hide nor hair of Dickens,' said Shetland Tony, 'but I'll tell ye what, if we do hear anything we'll let ye know – I'll get a wee message to you through the Company of Fishmongers.'

'Thanks,' said Molly. 'Nice *Blind-Man's-Buff* caper, by the way.'

With that, Shetland Tony gave Her Majesty a friendly pet, and he and his gang sauntered off down the laneway with full pockets, leaving Molly and her friends with the two gentlemen who were still sitting in the dust, pushing and pulling at the bowler hats that were jammed fast over their eyes.

'I … I say, Bounderby,' said the first man, pulling at his hat.

'What is it you say, Caddsworth?' said the second man, pushing at the brim of his bowler.

'I say,' said the first man, 'what a jolly rum show!'

The second man's hat suddenly POPPed off his head. He was bald and had a beard but no moustache. 'Yes, indeed,' he said, 'as you say, that show was most rum.'

The first man's hat came off with a similar POPP; this man was bald like the other, but in contrast to the first, he had a moustache and no beard.

Molly and Bram looked at each other in disbelief.

'Bounderby!' said Bram.

'And Caddsworth!' said Molly.

The two diminutive men on the ground rubbed their eyes and looked up at Molly.

'Girl,' said Bounderby slowly.

'Red hair,' said Caddsworth with a gulp.

'Blue dress,' said Bounderby, his small eyes wide.

'These,' said Harry Dickens with a groan, 'are the two detectives Ellen and my sisters have hired to find my father – I told you they were absolute idiots.'

'Oh, I *know* they are eejits,' said Molly, 'we've met them before, back when they tried to kidnap me in

Dublin.' The two detectives scrambled to their tiny feet; they were barely taller than the children.

'So sorry about that, old chap,' said Caddsworth.

'Oh yes, indeed,' said Bounderby, 'so sorry about that; we were only following orders, don'tcha know.'

'And what about your orders to find my father?' asked Harry. 'Is there any word on where he might be?'

'Ah,' said Bounderby, 'early days yet, Master Harry, I'm afraid.'

'We just visited this tavern, *Ye Olde Cheshire Cheese*, because we heard your father sometimes frequented it for writing duties,' said Caddsworth.

'We were looking for clues,' said Bounderby, 'but I'm afraid we had to leave quite suddenly.'

'Yes, indeed, as you say, Bounderby, we simply *had* to leave quite suddenly,' said Caddsworth. 'You see there was a strange green creature of the avian variety.'

'A *flying* green creature,' said Bounderby, 'with feathers and an objectionable vocabulary.'

'To wit,' said Caddsworth, 'a rude parrot.'

'Indeed, Caddsworth,' said Bounderby, 'an extremely rude parrot. You see, this rude parrot …'

'It POOHED ON MY HAT!' wailed Caddsworth. He held up his headwear, the crown of which was smeared with slimy white streaks. To Bram's eye the top of the bowler hat resembled the head of Horatio Nelson's statue, which stood atop Nelson's Pillar in Dublin's Sackville Street and was perpetually covered in seagull poo.

After bidding Harry and his new friends farewell, the two detectives dusted themselves down, turned on their miniature heels and left to continue their bungling search for the great author.

'What did I tell you?' said Harry. 'A pair of absolute idiots. Now you see why I resolved to search for my father by myself.'

'And what did *I* tell *you*?' said Molly. 'You're not by yourself – you have us!'

Molly tied Her Majesty's leash to a drainpipe beside the door to *Ye Olde Cheshire Cheese*, and the three children entered the tavern.

The taproom of *Ye Olde Cheshire Cheese* was snug and cosy, with mahogany panelled walls on each side, and several patrons sitting alone at separate tables, their flat caps pulled low on their heads. On the

opposite wall to the door was a great sooty fireplace in which, despite the summer warmth, a small
fire was lit, and small flames danced and crackled
in the grate. Beside the fireplace was a wooden bar
counter with shiny metal taps for pulling pints of
ale, behind which was a portly barman who seemed
to be having a somewhat heated discussion with a
disgruntled customer on the other side.

'I'm tellin' ya,' said the angry customer, his face
red, 'vat fing's a *game of lawn tennis*!'

'A *game of lawn tennis*?' whispered Molly to Bram.

'Cockney rhyming slang,' said Bram. 'I think he's
saying that something is a *menace*?'

'It's after doin' its business in me *slug an' snail*!'
continued the man holding up his pint of ale. The
top of his pint looked extra creamy, and Bram pulled
a disgusted face as he thought about Caddsworth's
hat and realised what the extra cream in the patron's
pint might be.

Suddenly there was a loud SQUAAAWWKK!
from behind them, and a green feathery shape
swooped low over their heads. Instinctively, all the
customers in the tavern ducked their heads and cov-

ered their pint glasses with their hand. 'LUBBER-WORT!' screamed the shape. 'MUCK-SPOUT! PAY UP, YOU MEAN OLD TALLY-SWERVER!'

'That's Myrtle,' said Harry. The parrot swooped over their heads again, this time raking its claws through Molly's red curly hair. The man at the bar shook his fist at the bird. 'I want a new *skating rink*!'

Myrtle flew across the room again and settled on the mantelpiece over the fireplace, where she perched happily, grooming her green feathers and muttering a series of bad words to herself.

'Father usually sits over there to write, when he's in,' said Harry, pointing to the table to the right of the fireplace. While Harry went to talk to the barman, Molly and Bram walked over to Dickens' favourite writing spot, giving the wild bird a wide berth, and searched under the seats and around the table. They checked the coal scuttle beside the fireplace and even looked behind a big painting of an old-fashioned gent in a curly wig that hung from the mahogany wood panelling. They found nothing at all, expect for dust, two spiders and a great number of smallish green feathers that they imagined must have fallen from Myrtle. A couple more feathers drifted down from the mantelpiece as the bird groomed itself.

Suddenly the green parrot on the fireplace SQUAAWWKed again, making Molly and Bram jump; they had almost forgotten she was there. 'FUSTILUGS!' screeched the bird. 'FUNGUS-SNOTS! BAH HUMBUG!'

Harry sat down beside them. 'I talked to Jenkins, the barman,' he said. 'He says Father hasn't been in here for weeks, just like I thought.'

'GUBBER-DRAGGLE!' squawked Myrtle. 'TAKE 'IM UP TO JACOB'S!'

'The green feather we found on the stage in the Lyceum must mean *something*,' said Bram, speaking loudly to be heard over the manic squawking. 'It didn't get there by itself. Maybe whoever took your father came the Ye Olde Cheshire Cheese looking for him and then when they couldn't find him here, went to the place where they knew he definitely would be, the Lyceum Theatre. It was well known he was doing a public reading there last night, I dare say.'

The parrot SQUAWKed again. 'MR GRIM-BLE!' it shrieked. 'GRAB 'IM! TAKE 'IM UP TO JACOB'S ISLAND!'

'Oh my goodness,' said Bram, exasperated, 'doesn't that parrot ever pipe down?'

'YES, MR BLEAT!' said Myrtle the parrot, in a shrill voice. 'TO JACOB'S! GRAB 'IM!'

'Wait!' cried Molly. 'Harry, you said this parrot has a bit of a bawdy beak on her?'

'Yes,' said Harry, 'you can hear her yourself – she never stops with the bad language and name-calling.'

'She certainly is the foulest of fowls,' said Bram with a smirk.

'MR GRIMBLE!' shouted the parrot. 'YOU PERISHING CHUMP!'

'But,' said Molly urgently, 'you *also* said Myrtle sometimes repeats what people say?'

'I …' said Harry, his eyes widening, 'Oh MY! What has she been squawking about? Maybe … maybe she's overheard something!'

They looked up at the parrot on the mantelpiece. Myrtle fluffed up the feathers on her wing with her yellow beak and looked back at them.

NOTICE:

MR G. TAYLOR, THE MANAGER OF THE

LYCEUM THEATRE
WELLINGTON STREET, LONDON

WISHES TO BRING TO YOUR ATTENTION

A PUBLIC PERFORMANCE

BY MR

CHARLES DICKENS

Mr Dickens will read from
his most remarkable novel

"A CHRISTMAS CAROL"

on the evening of

FRIDAY, 24TH JULY
AT 8 O'CLOCK

TICKETS AVAILABLE AT THE DOOR

GOD SAVE THE QUEEN!

'GRAB 'IM!' she squawked. 'GRAB CHARLIE! WE'LL TAKE 'IM UP TO JACOB'S ISAND!'

'Jacob's Island ...' said Harry, standing up.

'That's across the River Thames, I think,' said Bram, taking out his map of London and uncrumpling it on the table, 'nearly opposite the Tower of London; I recognise the name because it's mentioned in *Oliver Twist*.' He looked at Harry, 'That's where your father did away with the bad guy in the book, Bill Sykes. Maybe Jacob's Island where your father is being held!'

Molly raised a hand to pet the parrot. Myrtle nuzzled her green-feathered head into Molly's finger and squawked gently. 'Thanks, Myrtle,' said Molly, 'keep up the good squawking!' She turned to the others. 'Right,' she said, 'which way to Jacob's Island?'

Chapter Nine:

·······································

I'm So Sorry, Mr Dickens Is
Tied Up At The Moment

The great author's nose was terribly itchy. He desperately wanted to sneeze, but didn't dare to. His reluctance to let go with an almighty *pickle and cheese*, as the thugs who kidnapped him would say, was down to two factors. Factor number one, his hands were tied behind his back, and two, his head was completely covered with a hood, a hood the famous writer decided had probably served as a dirty laundry bag in the not-too distant past – it certainly smelled of old stockings and underpants. If he sneezed inside that hood, it would cause the most awful mess.

'I say,' he said, 'I say, Mr Grimble, is it? Or Mr Bleat? I wonder if one of you gentlemen could possibly lift this cloth covering off my head, even just for a moment?'

Hearing no reply, he went on, 'Halloo? I'm afraid I may have to – oh! – *aaahh.*'

Through the stinky material of his hood, the author could hear the muffled noise of footsteps drawing closer.

'AAHHH!'

The footsteps sped up.

'AAHHH!'

Two rough hands grabbed the bottom of the hood and pulled it upwards off the great author's head, just in time for –

'CHOOOOO!!'

After he had rubbed his eyes and allowed them to adjust to the dim light of the room, Charles Dickens found himself looking into the shocked, somewhat sodden face of a huge, thuggish man. The man's nose was bent sideways, as if it had been badly mushed more than once in bare-knuckle boxing matches, and his eyebrows looked as if they were formed from hedgehog quills rather than human hair.

'Ha!' came a voice from behind the man. 'Mr Grimble! Ol' Charlie's gone and done a *pickle an' cheese,* an' now your *boat race* is dripping with *sailor's knots!*' Mr Grimble uttered a low growl and wiped his snot-covered face with the hood. The other man, slightly smaller in height than the first, but considerably wider, continued laughing until Mr Grimble fixed him with a ferocious stare. The second man cleared his throat and looked away, pretending to whistle a tune.

Dickens looked around the room he was being held in. The walls were filthy and bare, with exposed bricks showing through crumbling plaster. The only light came from stubby, half-melted wax candles that were dotted here and there, and the room's solitary window was boarded up with rough planks of wood, inexpertly nailed together with bent iron nails.

'I wonder,' said Dickens, 'if either of you gentlemen would be so good as to tell me where I am? Or, failing that, why you have – a-hem – abducted me?'

Mr Grimble smiled, showing a row of green teeth, several of which were chipped and broken. 'Shall we tell 'im, Mr Bleat?' said Mr Grimble. 'Shall we tell 'im the reason why we kidnapped the world's most famous-est *biscuit-biter*?'

'I beg your pardon?' said Dickens. He thought he was well-versed in Cockney rhyming slang, but this was a rhyme he hadn't heard before.

'*Writer*, Mr Dickens,' said Mr Bleat, 'ain't that right, Mr Grimble?'

Mr Grimble nodded menacingly and smiled again. Dickens thought the man's teeth looked like a row of broken windows in a derelict dockside warehouse. 'Would *you* like to tell 'im, Mr Bleat?' he said.

'No, no, Mr Grimble,' said Mr Bleat, 'I am just an 'umble servant, you are the one with the *drift of the crab*.'

'I'LL TELL HIM!' came a loud, imperious voice from behind them.

Dickens looked up to see a tall, broad-shouldered woman, dressed head-to-toe in black. She wore a long gown with a black bustle to the rear, and her hands were clad in black lace gloves. On her head she wore a black hat, topped with black fabric roses, and her face was covered with a black lace veil. Over one black forearm was slung a cage-like black hand-bag, in which sat a miserable-looking white cat.

'MR DICKENS!' she bellowed, making the poor author flinch back in the wooden seat he was tied to. 'For many years I have loved your work. I have read everything you have ever written – from *The Pickwick Papers* to *Oliver Twist* and from *Martin Chuzzlewit* to *Little Dorrit* – every story, every chapter, every paragraph. My hungry eyes have consumed every word, every syllable and every letter. I have delighted in every semi-colon and have devoured every full stop. I have breathed in every scene and every character. I have feasted on your work.'

'Oh,' said Dickens, 'how nice.' At a gesture from the woman, Mr Grimble pulled a seat over and she sat down opposite Dickens with the caged cat on her lap and stared hard into Dickens' lined face with piercing eyes behind her black veil.

'I'm afraid you have me at a disadvantage, madam,' said the great author, with a small smile. 'You know me, of course, but I don't believe we've been formally introduced.'

'I am Lady H,' said the woman, her nostrils flaring under the lace, 'that is the only name you will require. As to *what* I am, I thought I was making myself quite clear: I am your greatest admirer. Your very GREATEST admirer. I consider your work to be almost perfect,' she growled, 'and you will note that I say *almost*.'

Dickens raised an eyebrow. He reached out a hand to pet the white cat; it looked so sad and neglected in its little black cage, and Dickens was so terribly fond of animals.

'DON'T TOUCH IT!' roared Lady H. 'You will MOLLYCODDLE it and SPOIL it!' Both Dickens and the cat recoiled, as if by the force of an exploding gunpowder keg.

'Do you know *why* I consider your work to be *almost* perfect?' asked Lady H.

Dickens, dumbfounded, shook his head mutely.

'Because,' continued the woman, 'of *The Old Curiosity Shop*.'

The Old Curiosity Shop? thought Dickens. Why, it was almost twenty years since he had written that book! It was all about a young girl called Nell who lives with her grandfather at the Old Curiosity Shop from the book's title – they fall foul of an evil moneylender and run away to the country, where poor sickly Nell dies and the grandfather withers away in sorrow. It was a very sad book, but happily for Dickens, it sold thousands-upon-thousands of copies. Like the book he was working on (or should have been working on, if he hadn't been kidnapped), *The Old Curiosity Shop* was published monthly, and his readers were so caught up in what was going to happen to little Nell, there were near riots outside bookshops and newsagents when the last number went on sale. It was a fun book to write, he remembered, and he was perfectly happy with the sales figures. Everybody is entitled to their opinion he supposed, but still he had no idea at all why this Lady H should only consider it *almost* perfect. *Unless* …

'YOU. LET. LITTLE. NELL. DIE!' shouted Lady H.

Dickens opened his mouth to speak, but Lady H silenced him with a glare.

'That,' said the woman, 'is why I have brought you here.' She clicked her fingers; at once Mr Bleat came forward with a small mug containing several pencils, and Mr Grimble sidled over with a pad of paper. 'Undo his hands,' Lady H demanded, setting down her captive feline companion. The two henchmen hopped to her command.

Dickens rubbed his wrists with his hands and stretched out his stiff arms.

'You see, Mr Dickens,' said the woman, 'you may have created these characters – the Pickwicks, the Oliver Twists, the David Copperfields, the … poor little Nells – but once those stories are out in the world, once people read them, experience their lives and live their experience, the characters become part of the public consciousness. You, Mr Dickens, do not own these characters anymore; no, no – they belong to the reader.'

Lady H reached up and pulled back her veil, revealing a sturdy face with two bright, piercing eyes in which Dickens could sense huge reserves of both sadness and terrible anger.

'*I* am the reader,' said Lady H, 'and I will not accept that little Nell is dead!'

She flung the paper and pencils onto Dickens' lap.

'You will not rise, sir,' she said in a cold voice, 'until you have rewritten the ending to *The Old Curiosity Shop*. I wish, sir, to have an ending where LITTLE NELL DOES NOT DIE!'

With that she whipped up her caged cat from the floor and marched out the door, slamming it behind her.

Dickens sat back in his seat, holding the paper and mug of pencils. He looked up at the two burly henchmen, his mouth open and his whole face a question mark.

'Well, Mr Dickens,' said Mr Bleat, 'you best get to re-writing that book, isn't that right, Mr Grimble?'

'Indeed it is, Mr Bleat,' said Mr Grimble, 'he best get to re-writing that *thief and crook*, because uvverwise …'

'Otherwise?' stuttered Dickens.

'Because uvverwise,' said Mr Bleat, 'Lady H has given us orders to break your *scrambled eggs.*'

'That's right,' said Mr Grimble, '*both* of 'em.'

CHAPTER TEN:

I WANT TO TAKE YOU
TO THE ISLAND

IN WHICH MOLLY, BRAM AND HARRY STOP BY A STINKY ISLAND,

AND MEET A BOY FROM THE HIGHLANDS

Jacob's Island was across the Thames on the southern bank in an area known as Bermondsey. Bram, Molly and Harry had to walk up the slope to St Paul's Cathedral and then pass through a maze

153

of smaller streets and alleyways until they reached London Bridge, where they could cross the river.

'There's no island here,' said Harry as they walked through streets bordered by dilapidated warehouses and derelict factories, 'there's just a small river, the Neckinger, more of a stream really. It's mostly underground, but it flows out here into the Thames.' Harry sniffed the air, then pinched his nose between his fingers. 'They say it's the most polluted river in England – every drain and sewer between Bermondsey and Southwark empties into it.' They looked down into the river; it flowed sluggishly, its brown water thick and stinking. Here and there rats bobbed up from the mire, took a lungful of smelly air, and dove back down into the porridge-like water again.

'It's a bit like the Poddle,' said Molly to Harry. 'That's an underground river back in Dublin that flows into the River Liffey. This Neckinger river is much stinkier than the Poddle, though – it's like someone turned the Poddle into piddle and poo.'

Her Majesty whined and wiped at her snout with her doggy paws; she didn't like the smell either.

The wooden buildings at the side of the river were tall and rickety; a couple of them, with broken windows, ramshackle balconies and gaping holes in their roofs, leaned precariously in over the river, looking like divers about to launch themselves off a high dive board into the pool below.

Despite their derelict and abandoned appearance, ragged items of clothing hung from frayed washing lines that were strung between some of their balconies and windows.

'My goodness,' said Bram, 'people *live* here?'

Harry nodded gravely. 'Oh, yes,' he replied, 'if you can call it living.'

Bram had seen deprivation in Dublin; his home city was infamous for its terrible tenements and slums – Molly herself used to live in a shack on the banks of the Royal Canal – but even the most desperate of Dublin hovels couldn't compare to the levels of hardship and destitution that London had to offer. Molly's shack, thought Bram, may have been tottering and tumbledown, but at least it was cosy and homely. The buildings here at Jacob's Island couldn't be described as homely. Not one window had as much as a candle lighting behind it, and not one single decrepit house-hold had as much as a solitary wisp of smoke coming from its crumbling chimney stack. Even though it was high summer in London, if felt as though the Island was shivering under a biting rime of winter frost; it was cold, neglected and unwelcoming.

'These are the places that my father is always trying to raise money for,' said Harry. 'He is continually trying to show people how the poorest of the poor have to live. You were right, Bram, he even mentioned Jacob's Island in *Oliver Twist* – this is exactly where the bully boy Bill Sykes got his comeuppance.'

A tiny girl, dressed in rags, came out of a decaying doorway of one of the buildings and made her faltering way across a flimsy, handmade wooden bridge that crossed the muddy river to a building at the other side, her small hands on a greasy rope that served as a guard rail.

'Halloo!' called Molly. 'Little girl!' The small figure kept moving, her eyes down. 'Hallo! We just want to ask you a couple of questions!' said Molly. The girl stopped and the nailed-together planks she was standing on wobbled precariously.

'I say,' said Bram, 'would you happen to know a gentleman by the name of, emm … Mr Grimble?'

At the mention of the name the small girl's eyes opened wide and her mouth formed an O-shape of shock. 'Oh! No, sir,' she muttered, 'I never 'eard of 'im, sir – I'm a good girl, I am!' She put her head down and hurried across the broken-down bridge, disappearing into the darkness of an opening on the other side. Molly, Bram and Harry looked at each other; that girl had most definitely recognised the name of *Grimble* – they were on the right track.

'Hey, you,' said a deep voice from behind them, 'Malone, M., Stoker, B. and the Atrocious Harry Pee – I did'nae ken I'd be seein' ye again so soon!'

'Shetland Tony!' cried Molly in surprise, turning to greet the small gang leader. 'And the Long Acre Lads … and Lassies!' The girl to Shetland Tony's right nodded her head and winked at Molly, who winked back.

'Tony,' said Bram, 'we heard a name when we were in *Ye Olde Cheshire Cheese*, and something about Jacob's Island.'

'Aye, they're a tight bunch in the *Cheese*,' said Tony, 'thick as thieves as they say. I'm presumin' old Myrtle was shootin' off her beak?'

Bram smiled; he'd remember that foul-mouthed fowl for a long time.

'Ye said ye heard a name,' said Shetland Tony, 'what was the name ye heard?'

'It was Grimble,' said Harry, 'Mr Grimble – and I'm the *Astounding* Harry *Dee*, by the way, not the *Atrocious* Harry *Pee*!'

'Gwimble?' said one of the other Long Acre Lads. 'Oh, Shetland, vat Gwimble's a wight sort an' no mistake!'

'Yeah,' said the third boy, 'he 'angs around wiv vat uvver 'ooligan, Mr Bleat!'

'The two a' vem's bad news,' said the girl, shaking her head, 'vewwy bad news.'

'You think that those two *Sassenachs* have somethin' to do with your Mr Dickens being kidnapped?' asked Shetland Tony.

'Yep,' said Molly, 'we got Grimble's name straight from the parrot's beak.'

'Ah'm sorry, lassie,' said Tony. 'Ah'm afraid I cannae help ye. Grimble and Bleat may not be the two brightest buttons on mah grandad's sporran, but they are two of the roughest, toughest, HUGE-est, most dangerous boot boys that ye could ever have the bad luck to meet. Mah-self and the Long Acre Lads and Lassie are way too wee to go up again' them. We can tell you where they are – where their hideout is – but I warn ye, Molly, don't try to take 'em on; if mah gang is too wee, then your gang is too upper-class lah-di-dah.'

Molly opened her mouth to argue, then looked over at Bram and Harry – both were wearing well-made, tailored jackets and trousers, as well as shiny leather shoes. Bram had a black tie on and even Harry's top hat, as battered as it was, was clearly an expensive make. She looked down at her own dress; it was fashionable and finely-cut, so different to the shabby dresses and pinafores she wore when she used to be a full-time pickpocket and part-time fishmonger. She sighed. *Is that really the way Shetland Tony sees me*, she asked herself, *as an upper-class lah-di-dah young lady? Well, maybe that's what I'm becoming … but I'm still a champion sneak thief and a fishmonger at heart!*

NOTICE:

○

ENGLAND'S, NAY THE WORLD'S, FINEST AND MOST FAMOUS AUTHOR, MR CHARLES

DICKENS
REMAINS
MISSING

○

MR DICKENS WAS LAST SEEN AT THE LYCEUM THEATRE ON THE EVENING OF FRIDAY THE TWENTY-FOURTH OF JULY

○

HIS FRANTIC FAMILY HAVE OFFERED A LARGE REWARD FOR ANY INFORMATION LEADING TO THE RECOVERY OF SAID MR DICKENS

○

PLEASE MAKE URGENT CONTACT WITH THE DICKENS FAMILY AT GAD'S HILL PLACE, HIGHAM, KENT OR WITH HIS LOVING SON, MASTER HENRY 'HARRY' DICKENS, CURRENTLY AT FORTY-EIGHT DOUGHTY STREET, LONDON

GOD SAVE THE QUEEN!

'That's it!' she said, a smile creeping over her face. 'Tony, I know you can't help us, an' I don't blame yiz – the enemy is far too big and far too strong for both of our gangs together – but think I know someone we can call on.'

'Who is that, Mol?' asked Bram, 'Who can we call on, here in London?'

'Who we gonna call?' said Molly. 'The Worshipful Company of Fishmongers – that's who!'

CHAPTER ELEVEN:

THE OLD CURIOSITY FLOP

IN WHICH CHARLES DICKENS RELUCTANTLY READS OUT SOME
UNNEEDED ALTERATIONS

'A-hem.' The great author cleared his throat and, in the flickering candlelight, held the manuscript close to his face with graphite-stained fingers. Normally he adored doing dramatic readings of his works, and his audience usually adored him for doing them, but this time he thought that his current audience, consisting of two huge, muscle-bound, twisted-nosed henchmen, may not be quite as willing to give him a standing ovation as his regular audience would.

'C'mon, Charlie,' growled Mr Grimble, 'gerron wiv it!'

'And don't be expecting no *crash-landing carnation* when you've done,' said Mr Bleat. 'We're stayin' sittin' in our *meet an' greets*, ain't we, Mr Grimble?'

'Nor no *munch of showers* ee-vah,' said Mr Grimble. 'In fact, you won't be gettin' any congrat-u-ma-lations from us at all – it's Lady H you gotta please wiv this rubbish, not us.'

Charles Dickens cleared his throat one more time and, after wiping his brow with a silk handkerchief from his pocket, held up the paper with his untied hand and began to read.

'*Waving them off with his hand*,' he said in a tremulous voice, then stopped. 'This is the bit,' he said to the two thugs, 'where they all come in to see Little Nell – Kit, Nell's grandfather, the schoolteacher, all of them – and they think Nell is sleeping.'

'We know,' said Mr Bleat.

'We've read it before,' said Mr Grimble.

''Oo 'asn't?' asked Mr Bleat.

Dickens gulped quietly and continued.

'*Waving them off with his hand,*' he said, '*and calling softly to her as he went, he stole into the room. They who were left behind, drew close together, and after a few whispered words – not unbroken by emotion, nor easily uttered – followed him. They moved so gently, that their footsteps made no noise; but there were sobs from among the group, and sounds of grief and mourning.*

'*For she was dead. Or so they thought. There, upon her little bed, she lay, seemingly at rest. The solemn stillness was so like death, it caused her grandfather to cry out.*

'*"Oh! Nell!" he cried, "You have left me and gone up to heaven, like the angel you always was!" The old man covered his eyes in grief.*

'*"Why, no, Grandfather," came a voice from the bed, "I was only pretending to be dead all this time." The crowd in the small room gasped, and Nell's grandfather swooned into a nearby chair. "Ha, ha!" cried Nell, quite alive, "The joke is on you, Grandfather!"*'

Dickens looked up from his page. Mr Grimble and Mr Bleat were looking at each other, their battered and scarred faces unreadable in the candlelight. 'I dunno 'ow you do it, Charlie,' said Mr Grimble slowly, 'but I *hammer and spike* it!'

Mr Bleat nodded, 'I *like* it too; as a matter of fact, I *hand and glove* it!'

'NOOO!!!' roared Lady H from the doorway, 'I DO NOT LIKE IT, I DO NOT LOVE IT, AND I MOST CERTAINLY DO NOT BELIEVE IT! LITTLE NELL IS MUCH TO NICE TO PLAY SUCH A MEAN TRICK ON HER OWN GRANDFATHER!'

'Mr Dickens,' she snarled menacingly, 'write me a believable way of bringing Nell back to life or I will have my boys not only break both of your *scrambled eggs*, I will have them tear off your *garden shears* and blacken both of your *cottage pies*. Do you *Pablo Fanque's Fabulous Marching Band* me, Charles?'

Charles Dickens nodded; he had been given a crash-course in Cockney rhyming slang over the last few hours and, to his dismay, he could *understand* perfectly what Lady H was threatening him with. He gulped again, quite loudly this time and quickly picked up a pencil.

Chapter Twelve:

She Was A Fishmonger And Sure, 'Twas No Wonder

In Which Molly Asks For Assistance And Encounters Some Resistance

'Do you really think the Worshipful Company of Fishmongers will help us to find my father?' asked Harry, his voice trembling and low. Molly, Bram and Harry, with Her Majesty in tow, were hurrying back across London Bridge, busier now with the early evening traffic.

'It's the Fishmonger Code,' said Molly, picking up speed as she crossed the dusty bridge, dodging a horse-drawn carriage and swerving around a cart piled high with straw. 'Fishmongers help out other Fishmongers in times of need; and this is definitely *this* Fishmonger's time of need.'

'Fishmonger's Hall is just the other side of this bridge,' said Bram, checking his tattered London map as they scurried along. 'Look – I think that's it, there!' He pointed to a white stone building with short Roman columns and two rows of grand windows that was set low to the left of the bridge, down two flights of steps on the bank of the River Thames. The three friends bounded down the steps with Her Majesty following in their wake and raced to the large wooden entrance door. A gilded metal plaque beside the door read, *Fishmonger's Hall,* and below that, *Chapter House One, The Worshipful Company of Fishmongers, London Branch.*

'This is it!' said Harry excitedly.

Molly took a deep breath and smoothed down her dress. Beside the gilt plaque was a long metal chain;

Molly reached out and pulled hard on the chain, and somewhere inside the Hall, a bell tinkled. Molly, Bram and Harry exchanged nervous glances as the sound of echoing footsteps came from behind the door.

There was a K-KLIKK and the door opened with a long, low KREEEEAAAAAKKKK. 'Cod day to you,' said a tall, black-suited man. He nodded eagerly. 'COD day to you! Get it?'

The three friends looked at each other again, this time in puzzlement.

'Cod day! COD! Because we are the Company of Fishmongers!' The man looked disappointed that his young audience didn't seem to be enjoying, or indeed getting, his joke. 'Oh never mind, I'm just fishing for compliments.' He clapped his hands together. 'Fishing! For compliments! FISHING! Oh, never mind. What can I do for you?'

'We need to see the Master Fishmonger,' said Molly. 'I'm with the Hibernian Chapter and I need a teeny tiny little bit of help.' She made the same sign she had made to Shetland Tony when they had met the tiny thief that morning outside *Ye Olde Cheshire*

Cheese – she stuck out her thumb and bent in the index and middle fingers of her left hand, and at the same time she brought the little finger of her right hand up to touch her nose.

The butler straightened up immediately and made the same sign back to her. 'Of course,' he said, his voice less jovial and tinged with urgency, 'this way, if you please, young Miss.'

He led the three children and their dog into the tall, marble-walled entrance chamber and up a plush-carpeted flight of stairs which turned halfway up and led to a large, marble-floored landing. 'Wait here, please,' he said in a clipped tone and walked in a very military manner over to a tall oak door which he knocked on three times – two quick knocks followed by one slow knock. Bram glanced at Molly; she had used that knock before, she even had a similar whistle – two shrill, ear-splitting high-pitched notes and then one low, deafening bass note. *It must be the Fishmonger's Whistle!* he realised.

The butler opened the door softly, stuck his head around and exchanged muffled words with whomever was behind it. He straightened up again in his military way and, nodding his head curtly to the three friends, opened the door wide for them to enter, then took his place, standing to attention like a sentry, beside the door.

Molly, Bram, Harry and Her Majesty walked uneasily through the doorway. Each wall was panelled in rich, golden-coloured oak, and at the other end of the room were three arched windows that flooded the space with light. Every desk, table, shelf and window ledge was covered in statues of fish, some as small as a thumb and others as large as a sheep, and all of them made from gold, silver, bronze and other expensive metals. Each fish had eyes made of what looked to Molly's expert pickpocket eyes to be precious gems like red rubies, green emeralds and bright blue sapphires. The surfaces that weren't covered in fish statues and ornaments held stuffed fish that had once swum in the rivers and seas of England – Bram could see haddocks, herrings and mackerel, all stuffed with sawdust and mounted on wooden plinths, as well as larger specimens like tuna, swordfish and even a medium-sized shark. In the centre of the three windows was a large desk, the top of which was buried in yet more fish ornaments. Behind the desk was a large, bald-headed man with tiny, fish-like eyes. Over his grey suit he wore a blue apron with a wavy navy stripe stitched across the front, and his hands were covered with snow-white gloves.

'Speak thee thy name and rank,' said the bald man in a deep, sonorous voice.

'Malone, Molly,' said Molly firmly, 'apprentice level third grade with the Worshipful Company of Fishmongers, Hibernian Chapter.'

'What seek thee?' said the man. The large man's voice was so deep and low it seemed to make the windows vibrate in their panes.

'I call on the Worshipful Company of Fishmongers to come to the aid of a Fellow Fishmonger in her hour of need,' said Molly. 'Our friend has been kidnapped.'

'It's my father,' said Harry, taking off his topper, 'Charles Dickens!'

'You have to help us, sir,' said Bram. 'He's being held in Jacob's Island by two thugs; we have to rescue him – we promised Harry we would.'

The man's eyes shifted from Bram to Harry, and then back to Molly.

'Out of the question,' he boomed. 'The Worshipful Company of Fishmongers concerns itself with matters aquatic, not matters of artistic endeavour!'

'But isn't Dickens a matter for all?' pleaded Bram. 'Every fisherman has read *Oliver Twist* by candlelight as they while away the dark hours before dawn on their trawlers. Every fishmonger reads *David Copperfield* as he tots up the pennies from his till in the evening. Every street seller has a dog-eared copy of *The Pickwick Papers* stuffed into their apron. Dickens is for everyone! He writes about all of us! Whether you are rich or poor, a brave man or a coward … a fireman or a fishmonger – you will find yourself and *lose* yourself in Dickens' books.'

Molly looked at her friend in admiration; Bram certainly had a way with words. She knew that if Bram wanted to be an author, then that is exactly what he would be – nobody could stop him.

The large man blinked his small, dark black eyes. 'Impossible!' he blustered. 'We are all admirers of Mr Dickens and his work – of course we are – but I'm afraid the Worshipful Company simply can't intervene in matters not related to fishing.'

'Then,' said Molly, 'you leave me with no other choice – I hereby invoke Article Three of the Worshipful Fishmongers' Code.'

The man gasped and turned to look at his butler. 'You can't mean–' he stuttered.

'Yeah, I do,' said Molly. 'Article Three states that every fishmonger, in times of great danger or mortal peril, is entitled to receive one favour from the Worshipful Company of Fishmongers, a favour that MUST be granted without question. And after which, they will resign their Apprenticeship … and be a fishmonger no more.'

'You'd do that for my father?' said Harry in a small voice. Molly nodded solemnly.

Bram put his hand on Molly's shoulder. 'Are you sure about this, Mol? Your poor father and mother and your whole family were fishmongers before you; you can never be a fishmonger again – that's an awful lot to give up.'

She nodded again. 'Bram,' she said, 'you and the Spooks are my family now.' She pointed her thumb at Harry. 'Even this eejit here is like a second-cousin-twice-removed at this stage of the game. And nothin' is more important than family to me.' She nodded a third time. '*Nothing.*' She turned to the Master Fishmonger, her face set and eyes steely and bright, 'You ready for this?'

The large man closed his eyes, drew in a deep breath and held it, waiting for Molly to say the three most secret fishmonger words – a phrase that hid in plain sight, but yet held great power.

'I request that the Worshipful Company of Fishmongers aid us in findin' Mr Charles Dickens,' said Molly in in a steady voice, 'rescuin' him from the villains who have kidnapped him, and further request that the Company help us bring the writer back home to his family …'

'… ALIVE,' she continued, 'ALIVE. OH.'

Molly, without waiting for an answer from the Master Fishmonger, turned on her heel and marched out of the wood-panelled room. Bram nodded nervously at the huge man, and he and Harry, after doffing his topper once more, trotted after her.

'Master Fishmonger,' said the butler. 'I don't think the young lady quite grasps the fact that that Article Three of the Worshipful Fishmongers' Code only applies to favours that are directly related to fishing?' The large man shifted in his velvet-lined seat. 'Oh, I think she does, Mister Haddock,' he said in a low voice, 'that young lady is no fool.' He pursed his lips and tapped them with a finger. 'I should think that even now she is imagining a way of turning this crisis of hers – shall we say – fishy.' The large man stood. 'Haddock,' he said, 'get a man to follow them, we'd better keep a close watch on what's happening in this disappearing Dickens affair.'

A few minutes later Molly, Bram, Harry and Her Majesty were on London Bridge again, racing back towards Jacob's Island. 'Do you think they'll help us?' panted Bram as they jogged along.

'They better,' said Molly. 'I invoked Article Three of the Fishmonger's Code, and the Fishmonger's Code is not to be sniffed at. I know rescuin' Harry's Da isn't *exactly* fishin'-related, but … I might have something in mind for that.' She stopped running and stood with her arms against the parapet of the bridge, looking up the Thames toward Jacob's Island. The two boys pulled up beside her. 'Even so, boys,' she said, 'I think it might be no harm for the three of us to come up with a plan B – just in case.'

Harry took off his top hat and tapped it with his magic wand. 'I say,' he said breathlessly, 'if we are going to defeat these two huge thugs and heaven knows who else they have with them, and neither the Long Acre Lads nor the Company of Fishmongers are willing or able to help us, then I think I *may* have some equipment that might help us do the trick – the magic trick, that is – but we will have to go to my lodgings in Doughty Street to get it!'

Chapter Thirteen:

More Monkey Business

In which Billy the Pan pulls off a daring rescue and rallies his troops

The gorilla ROARRRed a ROARRR so strong and so loud that had Billy not been wearing his rusty metal saucepan hat it would have ruffled his hair; he felt the heat of the gigantic beast's breath on his face and scrunched his eyes. Hetty and Rose cringed away from the noise, which echoed off the walls surrounding the now mostly empty Smith-field Square. The two girls staggered backwards on the cobblestones and Hetty, tripping on a loose tent peg, ending up sitting on the dusty ground, a look of shock on her face.

The enormous ape turned on its muscular stubby legs and shuffled back through the ripped multicol-oured canvas of Madame Flo's fortune-telling tent. The children outside could hear crashing noises from inside the tent as the gorilla snapped heavy tent poles with its powerful hairy hands, followed by a SMASSHHH of shattering glass.

The sound of KLIPPing KLOPPing hooves, fol-lowed by a loud NEIGGHHHH! announced the arrival of Wild Bert. He pulled his horse Buttercup to a hurried halt and slipped off her saddle, land-ing on the cobblestones beside the group of children with his spurs jangling and his six-guns drawn.

'Flo!' he cried, tipping back his white cowboy hat and aiming his guns at the canvas wall of the half-destroyed tent. 'Lay low! I'm gonna shoot the varmint!'

'How can you shoot it?' said Hetty, still sitting on the cobbles. 'Them guns only fire blanks!' Wild Bert looked down at his guns; in his excitement he had forgotten that as a circus rodeo trick rider, pony-vaulter and sharp-shooter, he never ever loaded his guns with live rounds – he didn't even own any proper bullets. 'I guess I was frettin' so much about poor Flo,' he said, spinning each revolver around on his finger and slipping them smoothly into the bedazzled white leather holsters that hung from his gun-belt, 'that it plum slipped ma mind that ma guns are only props!'

'What are we gonna do, Billy?' whispered Shep, terror in his voice. 'Madame Flo and Calico Tom are trapped in that tent – with that massive monster!' He gulped and ran his fingers through his short black curly hair. 'An' it's gonna eat them up!'

Billy the Pan furrowed his eyebrows and took off his saucepan hat to scratch his head. *W.W.M.D.*, he thought, *What Would Molly Do?* Well, Molly always thought her way out of dangerous situations; she always used her head. Molly was the cleverest, brightest, most intelligent person he knew – Billy dearly wished that she were there, and he wished even more dearly that he might have been born with her brain-power. Billy didn't think he was clever at all; he knew he wasn't as brainy as Molly, and he feared he didn't have as much going on in the brain department as Hetty. He so wanted to protect his friends from danger, but all he had was his saucepan, his battered, bockity, rusty, trusty saucepan … and *maybe* that might just be enough.

He looked up. 'Bert,' he said, 'hand me your gun.'

'But Billy,' said Wild Bert, 'Hetty just reminded us that ma guns are loaded with blanks – they couldn't hurt a flea, let alone a huge monster like this here gorilla!'

'I don't need the guns to shoot,' said Billy, 'I just need them to make a bit of noise.' Wild Bert, a puzzled look on his face, whipped one of his revolvers from his holster and handed it to Billy. 'Right,' said Billy the Pan, 'let's see if we can get this gorilla to play follow the leader.'

Holding the gun by its barrel in one hand and his metal saucepan hat by the handle in his other, Billy approached the tent slowly. Bangs and crashes could still be heard behind the canvas. Using the metal handle of the revolver, Billy began to beat a loud

KLANGGing rhythm on the saucepan. KLANNGG KLANNGG KLANNGG went Billy's pan as he circled the fortune teller's tent. The crashes and bangs inside the tent came to a stop and Billy, over the noise of his KLANNGGing saucepan, could hear the huge gorilla's heavy, animal breathing.

A hairy hand came around the side of the multicoloured canvas, and the gorilla started to appear from the darkness. Billy the Pan moved off slowly, still beating out the KLANNGGing beat on his saucepan hat with the handle of the gun. The massive ape followed him, slowly shambling on its powerful, hairy legs. Billy led the beast toward the next tent along, a red sideshow tent owned by a carnival act known as Mangy Moe, the Dog-faced Boy.

Walking backwards as he KLANNGGed, Billy slipped through the canvas entrance to the Moe's tent. The gorilla followed him, seemingly entranced by the rhythm of the gun beating on the pan. As soon as Billy saw that the gorilla was in the tent, he stopped banging and, throwing himself on the ground, slipped under the canvas at the far end of the structure, emerging back out into the open air. The gorilla, inside the tent, resumed its rampage; Billy could hear canvas being ripped, chairs being smashed and a crunching noise that Billy thought may have been poor Mangy Moe's wicker dog basket being stomped on.

He sped back to Madame Flo's tent, putting his trusty saucepan back on his head as he ran. Wild Bert was already in the tent when Billy entered, standing amidst the destruction. Every one of Flo's red velvet wall-hangings was ripped to shreds, and every chair was broken to matchsticks. Even Madame Flo's crystal ball was smashed to pieces on the floor of the tent, the tiny shards of glass sparkling in the light from the rents and tears in the canvas. The only thing still standing in the tent was the velvet-cloth-covered fortune-telling table in the centre.

'Flo!' cried Wild Bert. 'Flo! Where are you at, honey bun?' The table at the centre began to shake, and then a small hand from underneath it pulled down the tablecloth to reveal, much to Bert and Billy's relief and delight, the small, cherubic face of Calico Tom. He scrambled up onto his feet and ran straight to Billy, who hugged him tight.

'Flo!' shouted Wild Bert as another figure unfolded itself from its hiding space beneath the table.

Madame Florence stood up and stretched, her hand massaging her lower back. Her flowing, midnight-blue gown was dusty, she was missing one large hoop earring and her purple turban sat askew on her head, its long orange ostrich feather bent in half – but she had a smile on her face as she walked over to her husband, Bert. 'I knew you'd save us,' she said to Wild Bert. 'I foresaw it.'

'Your crystal ball mustn't have been workin' even before that ape smashed it up,' said Bert, hugging his wife. 'It was good ol' Billy the Pan here that saved the both of you, not me!'

They all turned together as an almighty KRASSHH came from inside Mangy Moe's tent.

'Now we just need to capture this wild beast, so he doesn't hurt anyone else,' said Billy.

'She,' said Madame Flo. 'It's a lady gorilla.' She put the back of her hand to her forehead and closed her eyes in what she hoped looked like a mystical trance, 'It was my feminine intuition that told me …'

Billy smiled. 'A female ape?' he said. 'Well, then – I think I might *just* have thought of a plan!'

He ran outside to where Shep, Hetty and Rose stood; all were wringing their hands in worry. 'Flo and Calico are fine,' said Billy quickly, 'but don't relax yet – the gorilla is still on the loose and I've a couple a' missions for you to go on.'

'Hetty,' said Billy, 'I need you and Shep to pay a visit to The Marvellously Mystical Michelangelo Malvolio's workshop; I know he made Molly's travellin' trunk, but I think Magic Mick may be able to do us another favour. An' yiz better bring a cart with you.'

'Rose,' he said, 'I need you to go to Simon the tailor in King Street – he owes Molly a couple of favours too – ask him if he has any black material and some black buttons.'

'Flo,' said Billy, 'I know you're good with making clothes, do you think you could run somethin' up for me?' Flo looked down at the midnight-blue gown she had designed and sewn herself and nodded eagerly. 'Great,' he continued. 'And Bert, we are going to need some rope-twirlin' genius as well.' Wild Bert grabbed his lasso from Buttercup's saddle. 'You got it, good buddy! Yee-haaawww!'

'Lastly – Calico,' said Billy, turning to the tiniest member of the Sackville Street Spooks, 'I know you've been through a lot, what with that big ape tryin' to eat you, an' all, but you are *so* brave – maybe the bravest Spook of all! Do you think you could be brave again for me, one more time?'

'I'll be as brave as a lion that just escaped from Dublin Zoo, Billy,' said tiny Calico Tom in his remarkably deep voice, his little chest swelling with pride.

'Grand,' said Billy, 'This is what I want yiz all to do …'

* * *

Twenty minutes later, the Sackville Street Spooks assembled again by the carnival tents in Smithfield Square. The Square was now completely deserted of people and animals, the farmers and merchants having moved their herds of sheep, pigs, ponies, geese and goats quietly away while the gorilla was otherwise engaged, tearing up the sideshow tents. The

185

only people in the Square when the Spooks returned were a couple of police constables and a handful of navy-capped zookeepers, all of whom were hanging back and looking terrified as they gaped at the ginormous gorilla who was at that moment swinging from a high gas lamppost with one arm and beating her chest with the other.

'Careful,' said Billy the Pan as he, Hetty and Shep slid a long wooden box off the back of a horsedrawn cart, 'we don't want to scratch Magic Mick's lovely paintwork.' The tall sides of the box were decorated with painted mystical symbols and runes, as well as a picture of a shiny top hat with a white rabbit popping out of it. On the other side was a painting of a red-haired woman wearing a long red dress and holding up a spread of playing cards. Despite the danger, Billy had to admire Magic Mick's handiwork – he'd painted every diamond, club, heart and spade beautifully onto each card. 'Set up the magic box in the centre of the Square,' said Billy quietly, 'then all we need is Calico Tom – Calico, where are you?'

'Here, Billy,' said Calico Tom in his unusually deep voice. Billy turned to inspect him and grinned; the tiny boy was unrecognisable in his disguise. Calico was covered from head to toe in furry, black material.

'Cashmere,' said Calico. 'Simon the tailor said it's the finest he had!' On the boy's head was a quickly fashioned balaclava-style head covering that had an opening for his mouth so he could breathe, but instead of eye-holes there were two, bright, shiny black buttons.

'How do I look?' said Calico Tom. 'I can't see nuthin' with these buttons!'

'You look perfect,' said Billy. 'You look every inch a baby gorilla!' He turned to the others. 'Alright, does everyone know what they're doin'?'

Everybody nodded, and Wild Bert, lasso in hand, gave a quiet YEE-HAAWW.

'Right,' said Billy the Pan picking up a sack that lay beside the cobblestones and handing out its contents to the Spooks, 'let's go catch a gorilla.'

Rose led Calico Tom, who could barely see under his baby gorilla balaclava, to the door of the magic box where he sat, looking lost and forlorn.

Billy the Pan, Hetty, Rose and Madam Flo then slowly began to creep towards where the real gorilla was swinging on her lamp post, bellowing out deep, angry guttural noises. On Billy's signal, they began to beat out a regular rhythm on the saucepans he had given them from the sack with a selection of sticks, wooden spoons and metal ladles. KLANNGG KLANNGG KLANNGG KLANNGG, the repetitive beat rang out in the Square. The gorilla stopped shrieking and swinging and dropped down to the ground. She shambled towards the Spooks on her short, furry legs, and followed them as they walked slowly backwards, like a swarm of rats following a KLANNGing Pied Piper.

Led by Billy the Pan, the Spooks, with many quick, nervous glances behind them, moved slowly back toward the centre of the Square to where the Marvellously Mystical Michelangelo Malvolio's magic box stood. Still KLANNGGING their metal pots, they circled around the strong wooden box with the gorilla in tow, until the huge beast was standing directly in front of the box's door.

Billy, being the tallest of the Spooks, reached up to a small button towards the top of the box, artfully disguised as a diamond on a card that was floating over the head of the painted lady in the red dress. The door to the box silently slid across to reveal Calico Tom, sitting on the floor, dressed all in black and looking up with shiny button eyes. Under the balaclava, Calico opened his mouth, took in a deep breath, and issued a long, loud, lonely EEEEEEEEPPPPing noise.

At the sound of the EEEEEEEEEPPPP, the gorilla's huge head snapped around and she stared at Calico Tom. Calico made another EEEEEEEEEPPPPing noise, this one even more lonesome and plaintive than the last.

The gorilla's bright animal eyes grew wide at the sight of this small, black-furred creature, sitting all alone and seemingly abandoned. She reached out a long, furry arm toward the "baby gorilla" and tried to tenderly touch its chin with her fingers, but the 'baby' moved smoothly backwards into the wooden case. The gorilla followed it, stepping into the box with first one long-toed foot and then the other.

Hetty peeped around the side of Magic Mick's box. 'The primate's in the prison!' she hissed to Billy.

Billy quickly reached up and pressed the diamond on the playing card, and there was a soft

WHOOOSHHing noise as the box door slid shut again, closing the massive gorilla inside. 'Now!' shouted Billy to Rose, and the girl, already on her knees, pressed a small heart on a painted playing card close to the base of the box. Immediately, another door, this one half the size of the main door and hidden at the back of the box, slid open and Calico Tom slipped out, pulling off his baby gorilla balaclava. 'Janey Mack,' he said, 'I could hardly breathe in that yoke!' The door at the front WHOOOSHED open again, but the massive gorilla was nowhere to be seen – she had completely vanished.

'Ta-DAAA!' said Billy the pan, grinning at Calico Tom. Ignoring the banging noises that were coming from the hidden compartment deep inside the magic box where the gorilla was now trapped, Billy lifted up his steel ladle and KLANNGGed one KLANNGG on his lucky saucepan hat.

'YEEEE-HAAAAAWWWW!' yelled Wild Bert as he rode up on his white horse. 'Hi-Yo, Buttercup!' The rodeo trick rider was swinging his lasso around over his white Stetson hat and launched it towards the magic box, which was now shaking from side to side with each massive bang from within. The wide loop of the lasso plopped over the top of the box, and Wild Bert pulled hard on the rope, sealing the doors. With Buttercup's hooves clattering on the cobblestones, Wild Bert rode in circles around Magic Mick's box shouting 'YEEEE-HAAAAAWWWW!' at the top of his voice, until the box was wrapped up with loop after loop of rope, tighter than a bow.

He slowed the horse and, holding onto his white cowboy hat, sprang off its saddle and landed on the ground beside the box. 'Can I get a YAA-HOO?' he shouted.

'YAA-HOO!' shouted the Spooks together happily.

Madame Flo flew across the cobblestones toward the Spooks and threw herself into her husband's arms. The zookeepers and Peelers, sensing that the danger was over, approached the box cautiously and inspected it as it rocked back and forth with muffled grunts and gorilla noises coming from its innards.

'Well done, Billy,' said Flo. 'I have to hand it to you – what a great idea to trap a gorilla by enticing it with a baby one!'

'Arabella here just had a baby,' said one of the zoo-keepers. 'She left it behind when she escaped and must have missed it terrible – when she saw your little lad here dressed as the baby, she thought the baby was hers and went to get it; but … how did *your* baby escape?'

'This is a magic box that our pal The Marvellously Mystical Michelangelo Malvolio uses in his *Disappearing Lady* magic trick – the lady goes in, the door shuts, and when it slides open, the lady has vanished – the crowd gasps and breaks into applause!' said Billy the Pan. 'You see, there's another smaller box inside the box, it's on a turntable and it can spin around. Once the gorilla went inside the outer box to get at Calico Tom, the spinnin' box spun around and trapped her, Calico slipped out the back door, and Bob's yer auntie!'

'So,' said Hetty. 'The gorilla is safe and sound now, trapped in not one but two boxes.'

'Double wrapped for freshness,' beamed Billy the Pan.

'I have to hand it to ya,' said Hetty, clapping Billy on the back so hard that his saucepan hat almost fell off, 'that was a pretty good caper – it was almost exactly what Molly would have done.'

'W.W.M.D.,' said Rose,. 'It was kind of like the *Lost Baby* caper in reverse.'

'Maybe we could call it the *Lost and Found Baby Gorilla* caper?' suggested tiny Calico Tom in his gruff voice.

'All I wanna know,' said Wild Bert, 'is how those zookeepers are gonna get that heavy box, containin' the heftiest gorilla that this here cowboy has ever laid eyes on, back up onta that there cart?'

'We're goin' to help them,' said Billy the Pan, 'that's how.'

He nodded his head and rallied his troops, 'C'mon Spooks, we have work to do!'

'Aye, aye, captain!' shouted the Spooks, and got to work.

Chapter Fourteen:

A Tale Of Two Dickens

In which Molly & Bram prepare to fight, so that a father and son may reunite.

It was getting dark as the horse-drawn cab pulled up outside 48 Doughty Street and Molly, Bram, Harry and Her Majesty piled out. 'Would you wait here for us, please?' said Molly to the driver. 'We're only goin' to be a few minutes.'

194

Number 48 was a terraced house with three storeys over a basement, and there was a black-and-white tiled walkway up to the duck-egg blue hall door. Harry reached up and pulled the rope that rang the bell, and a few seconds later the door swung open.

'Oh, Master Dickens,' said the maid with relief in her voice, 'I was ever so worried about you – when you never come back from the Theatre this morning, I fancied you'd been kidnapped as well, just like your poor fa-fa-fa-faaath-er-er-er-er-er ...' She broke down into sobs. Molly and Bram looked at each other, both thinking the same thing – *Reminds me of our maid Lily back home.*

'Oh, Mabel,' said Harry, giving her arm a pat as he walked past her, 'please pull yourself together; Papa wouldn't like to see you blubbering.' He opened the door to the house's drawing room and ushered his friends inside.

The children were surprised to discover two small, bowler-hatted gentlemen already inside. Her Majesty gave a little whimpering bark that almost sounded like she was trying to say, 'Oh no, not these two eejits again.'

'Oh, good evening!' said Bounderby, sitting on a small armchair with a fine bone China teacup and saucer in his hand.

'Yes, indeed, Bounderby, a very good evening!' said Caddsworth, sitting on a small sofa drinking tea from a fine bone China teacup with his little finger in the air.

'Bounderby and Caddsworth!' said Harry. 'What are you two doing here? You're meant to be out searching for my father!'

'Ah, yes,' said Bounderby. 'That's what we've come to make our report on; isn't that right, Caddsworth?'

'Yes, indeed, Bounderby,' said Caddsworth, 'and our report is that we have found …'

'Absolutely nothing,' said Bounderby, 'There's no sign of poor Mr Dickens; we found no trace, we have no hint at all.'

'And we have no clue,' said Caddsworth.

'I always said,' said Molly, 'that neither of these eejits had a clue.'

'But *we* do!' said Bram. 'We know where Harry's father is, and you two are going to help us get him back!'

'We've a cab outside and we are all going straight to where Father is being held,' said Harry, 'but first we need to get a few things.' He got on his knees, pushed Caddsworth's legs out of the way and reached under the small sofa. After a bit of grunting and heaving, Harry pulled a big wooden box with a leather carrying handle from under the couch. He sat on the floor and opened the box. Inside was a large black metal object with a brass lens that looked a little like a large camera, but without the usual folding concertina snout. Harry opened a door in the side of the object and took out an oil lamp, giving the reservoir a shake to make sure it had oil inside it.

'It's a magic lantern' he explained to Molly and Bram. 'Once the oil lamp inside it is lit, this amazing machine can *magically* project images onto walls and surfaces – the effect is astounding – and these are the images we are going to project.' He reached into a pocket on the lid of the wooden box and took out a cloth envelope with writing on the front that was full of glass slides. Molly and Bram looked at each slide in turn, their eyes, and their smiles, widening with each one.

'Ooh,' said Molly, 'I think I see where you're going with this plan, Harry, and these yokes are perfect for it.'

Bram nodded. 'They couldn't be more fitting for your dad's rescue!'

Harry then opened the doors at the bottom of a mahogany bookcase and took out a bundle of black clothes, a large sheet of thin metal with a wooden handle at each end, and a cardboard box marked FIREWORKS. 'Papa calls this his thunder board,' he said handing the sheet of metal to Bram. 'Give it a try; hold it by the handles at each end and shake the middle up and down.'

Bram did as he was told. At once the room was filled with the ear-splitting sound of thunder. Her Majesty lay on the floor and put her furry paws over her ears.

'Don't worry, doggy,' said Molly, 'it's not really a storm, it's just the noise from the metal sheet!'

'Papa uses this for a stormy sound effect when he's putting on his family plays in the house,' said Harry. 'He writes them just for us, and all the family joins in and has a part. In his last play, I played this character.' He put on the outfit that was rolled up in the bundle: a black cape, a black mask with painted red dots over his eyes, and finally, a pair of shiny, patent-leather black boots. Each boot had a heavy metal spring attached to the sole.

'Spring-Heeled Jack!' cried Harry, attaching a smaller cape with a winged black collar onto Her Majesty's neck. 'And his spring-heeled dog, Savage!'

Bram looked at his gold-plated pocket watch; it was getting very late, and he was quite sure his parents would be wondering where he and Molly were. He fished around in his pockets for a pencil and a piece of paper. 'I say, Mabel,' he said to the maid, 'I wonder if I wrote a quick note, might you be so kind as to arrange to have it delivered to the Great Northern Hotel?'

'What are you going to tell them?' asked Molly, looking over Bram's shoulder as he scribbled.

'The truth,' said Bram. 'I'm telling Mama and Papa that we have an urgent appointment with Mr Charles Dickens!'

* * *

'Who on earth,' said Bram a few minutes later as the cab clattered over the cobblestones on its way back toward London Bridge, 'is Spring-Heeled Jack?'

'Jack is a creature that's meant to stalk the streets, haunting the rogues and the evildoers of London,' said Harry. 'He has a long black cloak, glowing red eyes and big, powerful springs on his boots. They say he can leap from rooftop to rooftop with his spring-heels, hunting criminals. He has his dog Savage with him, and the dog has red eyes too.'

'Heh,' said Molly, looking at Bram. 'It reminds me a bit of those vampire fellas you're always writin' stories about back home.'

Harry looked from Molly to Bram. 'Some say that Spring-Heeled Jack is an old wives' tale, something somebody invented to scare children, and he probably is, but if I know one thing about Cockney folk, it's that they are a notoriously superstitious bunch – Father always said so. If those two goons see me in this outfit, dressed up as the terrifying Spring-Heeled Jack with Savage at my side, it's bound to put 'em on the back foot!'

'Oh,' he said, tapping his topper with his magic wand, 'and, stroke of luck, Jack wears a top hat too!'

'Well, Master Dickens,' said Caddsworth, 'your costume certainly frightens me; doesn't it you, Bounderby?'

'Most certainly, Caddsworth,' said Bounderby, 'it positively gives me the shivers!'

'Does everyone know the plan, and what they have to do?' asked Molly, giving Her Majesty a pet. 'Or do we need to go over it again?' Everybody shook their heads; they all knew the plan backwards, and most of them, barring the naturally cowardly Bounderby and Caddsworth, looked eager to carry it out.

'Ho, there,' said the driver, pulling up his horses on the north end of London Bridge, 'this is as far as I go, gentlemen and young miss; cabs ain't safe on the other side of the river after dark – Bermondsey is choc-full of the criminal element; and pitch-dark too, as the people there are too poor to afford either gas lamps or candles. I don't wish to have my carriage wheels stolen again!'

They watched as the cab turned a wide circle on the now empty bridge and drove off to the bright lights and safety of the West End, and then they trudged through the moonlight towards the darkness of Jacob's Island, with Bram carrying the big box of fireworks, Molly manhandling the thunder board and Bounderby and Caddsworth hefting the big magic lantern box between them.

They were met at Jacob's Island, at the opening of the stinky underground River Neckinger, by Shetland Tony and the rest of the Long Acre Lads and Lassies. 'Och aye,' said Tony. 'Ah see you've gained a couple a' troops for yer army?'

'I say!' said Bounderby. 'It's him – the small chap who robbed us – I recognise his craggy Scottish accent!'

'It's him,' said Caddsworth, 'as you say, Bounderby – the wretch who stole my gold pocket watch!'

'And my new silk handkerchief,' said Bounderby.

'Now, now, detectives,' said Molly. 'Shetland Tony was only doing his job – he only steals to eat – isn't that right, Tony?'

'Oh, aye,' said Shetland Tony, quickly taking the new silk handkerchief from around his neck and burying the gold pocket watch deep in his pocket, 'I may be small, but I'm shockin' hungry ...'

'Alright,' said Bram, 'Tony, where are the two hooligans holding Dickens?'

Shetland Tony pointed to a room high up in the fifth storey of a wooden building that looked like it was going to totter over into the smelly, sludge-like river below. The window of the building was the size of a double door, with a rickety railing going across it at waist height. Over the door was a wooden beam with a heavy, fraying rope attached to it.

'That building used to be a warehouse, I think,' said Harry. 'The wooden beam with the rope is a kind of crane for winching goods up from river barges; that was when there used to be water in the Neckinger instead of slimy gloop – before it got used as a toilet by most of Bermondsey.'

'We need to get into the room below where Harry's father is being kept,' said Bram, pointing through the murky darkness to the window below the double doors.

'Aw, that'll be hard,' said Shetland Tony. 'We had a wee look earlier, an' they've got the whole place locked up as tight as a drum – ye'll never get in!'

'That,' said Molly, reaching up and removing a ring of shiny lock-picks from her curly ginger hair, 'won't be a problem.' Shetland Tony's eyes widened at the sight of the professional lock-picking kit that sparkled in the moonlight as Molly held it up.

'Aye,' he said in admiration of both the lock-picks and of Molly herself, 'I suppose it won't be, at that.'

After making sure that Caddsworth and Bound-erby had a pack of matches – they did, Shetland Tony and his gang hadn't stolen them – Molly sent the two detectives down to sit on a wooden walkway at the side of the river, directly underneath where the thug's window was, five floors above. They made their way gingerly across the ramshackle, rope-tied wooden bridges and walkways to their destination, carrying the box of fireworks between them.

'Remember,' hissed Bram as they wobbled away, 'once you hear the thunder, light one up; then another one or two every time you hear a peal of thunder after that!'

Carrying the magic lantern, Molly and Bram, with Spring-Heeled Harry and Her Majesty following, walked in the dim moonlight around to the other side of the building where they found a door, the lock on which Molly made quick work of. Once inside, they silently climbed the tumbledown steps up to the fourth floor and found the room immediately below the room that Shetland Tony reckoned that Charles Dickens was being held. Harry looked up at the ceiling of the room. They could hear the muffled creaking noises of somebody – or some *bodies* – walking around with heavy steps on the floor above them. 'To think,' he said quietly, his voice hoarse and angry, 'that my father is being kept up there against his will.'

'Don't worry, Harry,' whispered Bram, 'we'll get him out of there. Now, show me again how this magic lantern works.'

The three of them gathered around the box that contained the magic lantern and its slides. While Harry ran them though how it worked, they lifted the lantern out of the box and positioned it in the broken window of the room, with its lens pointed at the tall wall of the building directly across from them, on the other side of the slimy river. Harry used a match to light the oil lamp inside the machine and after a few moments, magnified by the glass in the lens, a strong beam of light emerged from the lantern. 'Pop the glass slides into this slot here,' he told them, pointing to a long, thin opening on the top of the lantern, 'and the beam will project it onto the wall over there. There are few lights in any of the buildings, and in this darkness the image should be very clear!'

'And with Bram's thunderbolts and the idiot detectives' lightning, it should also be very, very frightening!' said Molly.

'Good luck,' said Bram to Harry as the young magician fixed his topper on his head and bounced on his spring-heels across the creaky wooden floor to the door. 'Don't forget to wait for my signal before you do anything!'

Harry nodded gravely and, with Her Majesty dressed as Savage the spring-heeled dog at his side, made his bouncy way to the stairs to the next floor.

Molly counted to sixty and then looked out the broken window at the black, starless night sky. She craned her neck up to look at the wooden crane that jutted out over the thugs' window. 'He should be there by now, standin' right outside their door,' she said, looking back at Bram. 'Almost time to give the signal.'

* * *

In the room above, Lady H paced up and down, her anger growing by the minute. All she had wanted was a happy ending for little Nell, a believable one where the evil moneylender Quilp gets his comeuppance, and where Nell and her grandfather go back to *The Old Curiosity Shop* to live long and happy lives – was that too much to ask for? *Why* was Dickens not writing it for her?

'WHAT,' she shouted, her patience stretched so thin it resembled taffy being put through a mangle in a carnival candy stall, 'is the hold up? WHY am I not sitting here reading my new ending? WHY IS NELL STILL DEAD??'

Charles Dickens, his legs and his left arm tied to the same heavy chair he had been languishing in since that morning, gave her an apologetic look. 'I do beg your pardon, madam,' he said, his voice cracking though lack of water – neither the so-called 'lady' nor her two hired brutes had thought to give him as much as a glass of water or a cucumber sandwich since he had been kidnapped, 'but I'm sorry to say I can't for the life of me think of a believable way of bringing her back. The ending of *The Old Curiosity Shop* was rather good, some might say it was perfection itself – not me of course, your Ladyship, I would never stoop as low as to brag about my work – and I simply can't see how it can be improved. In fact,' he continued, 'I can't see very much at all by this candlelight; I'm afraid I can barely see well enough in this darkness to write anything at all.'

'Ol' Charlie's afraid of *a walk in the park*, eh, Mr Grimble?' said Mr Bleat.

'Oh yes,' said Mr Grimble, 'but ain't you afraid of *the dark* too? You always bring a lantern at night-time when you go to the lavvie to do your *old brown shoe*!'

'ENOUGH OF THIS!' screamed Lady H. 'Dickens, I have waited for years for my happy ending for Nell; I have been driven almost mad! Sometimes I thought I may end up in Bedlam! BEDLAM!! I have worn black and covered my face with a veil ever since

I read that cursed book and leaned of the poor mite's untimely death,' she continued, her head bowed. 'I have mourned that fictional unfortunate for nearly twenty years.' Estella, the small, sad white cat in the metal cage-handbag that Lady H habitually carried on her arm, turned as best she could in her confined space and mewled a mournful *meeewwwl*.

Lady H stood up, her wild anger rising to a feral peak. 'I wish to move on with my life, but I never shall until Nell is brought back – do so now, or you, like Nell, will find yourself in a pauper's grave, covered by six feet of worm-ridden soil, PUSHING UP THE DAFFODILS AND THE DAISIES!!'

Suddenly there was a deafening B-BOOOOM of piercing thunder outside the room, so loud it made the flimsy wooden walls shake. Plaster crumbled off in places with the vibrations of the noise and scattered like dust onto the filthy floor. Dickens raised his head and turned his neck around to look at the window. There was a sharp, intense burst of light outside, followed by a sizzling, fizzling noise, as if lightning had struck one of the buildings across the narrow river.

Lady H, her annoyance growing still further, marched toward the window and looked out, the handbag containing her poor, put-upon cat still on her arm. She gasped loudly and recoiled from the terrifying sight that greeted her widening eyes.

Across from her room on the wall of the building opposite was the looming, glowing figure of a tall, ghostly apparition. Its long body was covered in what looked like chains, its head seemed to be wrapped with a spectral bandage and its whole form shone with an unearthly luminescence. Lady H raised her black lace veil to get a better look, then immediately dropped it again in fear.

There was another ear-splitting thunder KKRASSHHH, followed by another fizzling, KRUNKKing flash of light. Lady H squeezed her eyes shut tight against the dazzle. When she opened them again, she was confronted by the image of another spirit, gleaming with radiant light. This spook wore a long, hooded cloak and was pointing an arm with a rotting, flapping sleeve and skeletal fingers. Lady H let out a small, shocked shriek of fright.

Dickens, exceedingly curious as to what was going on, craned his neck around. He greeted the ghost with a small, surprised smile of recognition.

Another thunderous B-BOOOOMMMMM sounded, perhaps the loudest of all. This time the lightning K-KRACKKED straight away, so bright and ferocious it lit up the dark room as bright as midday, and almost blinded Lady H.

The apparition changed to a glowing, undulating bent figure of a man with a bald head and an evil grin. In his hands he held a bulging bag of coins and a scroll with the word *DEEDS* printed upon it.

'Daniel … Quilp?' said the Lady, recognising the moneylender from her favourite novel.

'Ah,' whispered Dickens to himself, 'clever, clever …'

The last B-BOOOOMMMMM shook every ramshackle building on the stunted, smelly Neckinger River to the very foundations. Behind Dickens, Mr Grimble and Mr Bleat, both of whom considered themselves to be the very hardest of hard men, jammed their fingers in their ears and whimpered like scared puppies at the sound. The swizzling sparkles of the firework drifted down through a thick fog which cleared to reveal to Lady H, blinking and rubbing her eyes, a truly terrifying sight.

On the wooden wall across from her, floating in the air, was the radiant figure of a young girl. She wore a tattered dress, her feet were bare and she had a shabby bonnet on her head. Her arms were reaching out, as if to beg for help or assistance that would never come. The poor girl looked broken, grief-stricken and done for.

Lady H, walked forward blindly, reaching out her own arms toward the ghostly phantom. 'Little Nell,' she whispered, 'My poor, poor little Nell …'

The tall, broad-shouldered woman reached the waist-high wooden bar that served as a pathetic guard rail on the open doorway-window. With a splintering sound the bar cracked in the middle and bent out. Lady H tottered forward, her hands reaching out and grasping the clear night air. Estella the cat let out a loud, worried MIAOOOW as she swung out in her handbag over the stinky river five storeys below. Mr Grimble and Mr Bleat, seeing that their mistress was about to fall, moved dumbly towards her.

A last peal of thunder sounded, and the door to the room behind the two thugs burst open. They swung around to see their own demon – a monstrosity in a black, high collared cape with a top hat and red eyes glowing behind a black mask. On his black-shod feet were metal springs and beside him was a hell hound, its body covered by a flowing black cape.

'Yes,' said the wraith in a deep voice, 'it is I – Spring-Heeled Jack!'

Spring-Heeled Jack sprang into the room, as did Her Majesty with a loud bark. Jack threw down small white wraps of paper that exploded into clouds of grey smoke at the hit the floor. *Smoke bombs*, thought Charles Dickens, his smile glowing wider – he fancied he might be acquainted with the brave boy in this Spring-Heeled Jack costume! Mr Grimble and Mr Bleat most certainly were not aware of the identity of the boy in the costume; as far as they were aware, this was the real life, honest-to-badness Spring-Heeled Jack, and they flinched back from the KRAKKKs of the smoke bombs and the growling of the hell hound whose eyes glittered in the candlelight.

''Eaven 'elp us, Mr Grimble,' said Mr Bleat with sheer terror in his voice, 'it's old *King-Shield Quack* 'imself!'

'I sees 'im, Mr Bleat,' said Mr Grimble, his normally gruff voice now squeaky with fear. 'Oooh, I fink 'es going to cat us for his *fixer-upper*!'

Jack flexed his legs and made an almighty bounce toward them on his powerfully sprung heels; with high-pitched shrieks, they turned and ran past the seated form of Dickens toward the double doors where their mistress stood. They crashed through the already splintered wooden railing and fell with long, shrill screams to the river below. Dickens, even though he was tied up in a chair five floors above, could hear two squelchy splashes as the two hooligans-for-hire hit the thick, sludge of the polluted Neckinger River.

Lady H, the safety bar shattered and broken before her and her balance upset, teetered on the very edge of the open wooden double-doors with her arms still reaching out toward the vision of Nell. Estella screeched in her handbag-cage as the lanky Lady wobbled unsteadily and then lurched forward, falling into the night-air, her arms windmilling as she fell. One of her hands touched against the ancient rope that hung from the wooden crane beam, and she grabbed it and wrapped it around herself, swinging wildly from left to right.

In the room, Spring-Heeled Jack ran to Dickens and untied his legs and arm from the chair. The great author immediately used his freed arms to hug the infamous London demon as tightly as he could.

'Harry,' he said. 'My own dear Harry. I knew you would come to rescue your father – I simply knew it!'

Harry took off his red-eyed mask and, with bright tears in his real eyes, hugged his dear papa.

'Oh, my dog,' said Bram, as he and Molly firstly gawped out their window to where the two thugs, Mr Grimble and Mr Bleat, were being pulled out of the stinky river porridge by Bounderby and Cadds-worth, and then gaped upwards to where Lady H, with Estella on her arm, was dangling from an old, frayed rope. 'Mol, your plan worked splendidly!' Molly extinguished the oil lamp and took out the glass slide from the magic lantern's slot. At once the image of

Nell from *The Old Curiosity Shop* that had been pro-jected onto the building opposite disappeared. She put the slide carefully back into the cloth envelope marked WONDERFUL CHARACTERS FROM THE WORLD OF MR CHARLES DICKENS. 'It wouldn't have worked at all, Quality,' she said with a smile, 'without your terrifying thunder!'

Upstairs, with Harry holding on to one of his hands, Dickens leaned forward out of the open double doors and reached out towards Lady H. 'Give me your hand, madam,' he said. 'Swing to me, grab on to my arm and all shall be well!' He strained toward the swinging woman, leaning out as far as he dared, his fingertips almost touching hers, but to no avail – with a small cry, the woman lost her grip and began to fall. Estella the cat yowled as her handbag-cage flew off the woman's outstretched arm and tumbled into the air.

Suddenly a furry shape shot by Charles Dickens and Harry. It snapped at the handbag, catching the handle in sharp teeth, and then twisting its body around in mid-air and slapping its furry paws onto the ledge at the bottom of the double-doors. Using her claws to pull herself back into the room, Her Majesty opened her mouth and dropped the hand-bag-cage onto the dusty floor. Harry bent down to open the latch on the cage, and a very grateful Estella emerged, stretching her long feline body and arching her white furry back. As the two Dickens watched, the cat slunk over to where Her Majesty lay and nuzzled into her, thankful for the rescue and happy to meet her new friend.

'HEEEELLLLLLPPPPP!' came a loud voice from down below, causing the two Dickens and Molly and Bram to rush to their windows. 'HEEEELLLLLLPPPPP! I CAN'T SSWWIIIIIII-IIIIMMMMMMM!!' Lady H was frantically trying to swim in the thick, pungent, porridgey river goo, waving her hands as she slipped downwards into sludge. Rats, terrified by her loud screaming, swam and scurried right and left, launching their scrawny furry bodies up onto walkways and planks as they tried to get away from this new, black-clad river monster that had invaded their home.

'What shall we do?' said Bram, springing to his feet like Spring-Heeled Jack himself. 'We'll never make it to her in time – she'll drown in that awful river!'

Just then a loud voice sounded out in the midnight air, a strong voice that sounded three words in a clear tone: 'COCKLES AND MUSSELS!' It was joined by a multitude of voices, all with London accents, all shouting their reply, 'ALIVE, ALIVE, OH!'

'It's the Worshipful Company of Fishmongers!' cried Molly, watching from the window. 'They came!'

The Fishmongers, led by the large, bald-headed man with tiny, fish-like eyes, hurried to the side of the stinky river where Lady H was sinking below the slime, and cast a huge rope net into the thick water. Together they strained and pulled, their leader shouting, 'HEAVE, LADS, HEAVE!'

With a loud PLUUURRRPPP, Lady H's long, broad-shouldered form surfaced from the sludge and floundered up onto the bank, as the Fishmongers reeled in their catch. She lay on the filthy wooden planks the riverbank, wheezing and snorting, trapped in the Fishmongers ingeniously-knotted net. Their leader looked up to where Molly and Bram were hanging out the window. 'The Worshipful Company of Fishmongers, London Branch, at your service,' he shouted. 'As I said, we cannot intervene in any matters unrelated to fishing … but we are more than willing to stretch the rules to help a fellow Fishmonger *catch* a fish – no matter how big and black-clad it may be!'

'Cockles and mussels,' shouted Molly with a smile. 'Alive, alive, oh!' came the happy reply from the leader.

'You knew they'd help!' said Bram.

'No – I didn't,' said Molly with a grin, 'but I knew they'd be watching, and that they'd wade in if there was a fishing emergency of any kind – I was pretty sure *someone* would end up needing to get fished out of that stinky river. I'm just glad, Bram, that it was Lady H who needed rescuin', and not you or me!'

'Hey, there – you boy,' came a shout from above, 'What's today, my fine fellow?'

Bram, recognising instantly the quote from his favourite book – the book he still had tucked into his jacket pocket – looked up to see the smiling face of Charles Dickens looking down at him. Harry was beside him with his arm around Her Majesty.

'Why, it's after midnight, so it must be Sunday, sir!' replied Bram with a grin.

'Thanks for helping me find my father,' shouted Harry.

'And thank you both for helping my boy,' said Dickens. 'You are true friends to both me, and to my son. And what a performance, Harry, your best yet!' He hugged his son. 'Harry,' he said, 'you really are ... *magical.*'

Molly looked down to see fireman and police constables arrive to arrest the soggy and whiffy Lady H and her henchmen, all of them now trapped securely in the Fishmongers' huge net. She waved a wave of thanks to Shetland Tony and the Long Acre Lads and Lassies, who each waved a quick wave back, and then, giving a furtive glace to the approaching coppers, made themselves scarce.

The Diary of Master Abraham Stoker
Sunday 26th of July 1859
Great Northern Hotel,
London

Dearest Diary,
My sincerest apologies for two full days with no com-

munication — I dearly would have loved to write, but I'm afraid I simply couldn't find the time — myself and Molly have been quite busy rescuing authors and trapping thugs.

I won't go into the details tonight. As a point of fact, the present moment can actually no longer be described as night at all; as it's now past four o'clock, a more accurate description of the time at present would be morning.

But I'm rambling, Dear Diary! We are to head back to Dublin on Tuesday morning; perhaps I will find time either on the train or the steam-packet to update you more fully on our thrilling adventures in London.

Suffice it to say that I fear your pages may be (metaphorically) set alight by all the excitement!

Yours sleepily,

Bram.

Epilogue:

There's No Place Like Home ...

IN WHICH MOLLY & BRAM RECEIVE A ROYAL MESSAGE AND BID
FAREWELL TO A COUPLE OF FRIENDS

The next morning, Molly and Bram walked into the breakfast room of the Great Northern Hotel, scratching their heads and yawning – it had been a late night. They had to wait around to make statements to the police, then they had to bid a fond farewell to their new friend Harry and his tired but eminently talented father, Charles. Even when they got back to the Hotel, they had to knock on a back door to rouse the chambermaid who was taking care of Her Majesty; Elsie was a sound sleeper and had taken an age to appear at the door, but was over-joyed to see the dog, especially as she was still dressed in her brand new and very fetching Spring-Heeled Savage cape and collar. The friendly chambermaid had even seemed happy to see Her Majesty's new best friend Estella, Lady H's former feline prisoner, who stretched her long, white, furry body and trot-ted in through the hotel's back door after the dog with her tail held high. Molly smiled as she watched the cat nuzzle her feline face into Her Majesty's legs and found herself wondering if there was room inside her tricked-out travelling trunk for *two* pets.

'Hallooo, there!' said Bram's older brother Thorn-ley from where he was sitting at the breakfast table between Bram's mother and father. 'So nice of you two to join us!'

They sat down at the other side of the table. Molly dived into the food that was laid out, lifting the cov-ering on a silver platter of sausages and piling her plate high with eggs and bacon.

'Still have your appetite I see, Miss Malone?' said Thornley. 'I seem to remember you being starving the last time we met as well, when I was back for the Easter half-term.' Molly gave him a grin through a mouthful of delicious, juicy sausage – not even Thornley's snarky comments could bring down her good mood this morning.

'Of course,' continued Thornley, as Bram shot him a look, 'there's so little else to do in Dublin but eat. London is so much more exciting. I was just telling Papa, Bram, how the Withering Hall Under Fifteens won the rugby schools' cup, and how we were all so excited we pulled old Lumpy Snedderington from his bed and chucked him in the stream, nightgown and all, and chucked in his sleeping cap after him!' Thornley erupted in braying laughter. 'I bet nothing as exciting as that ever happened to you!'

Just then a remarkably nervous-looking waiter approached the table. His hands were shaking as he held a red velvet cushion, on the top of which was a folded piece of cream-coloured parchment.

'Mr Stoker,' he said in a trembling voice, 'it's, it's a letter from the Palace.'

'Ah,' said Papa Stoker gruffly, reaching for the letter with its shiny gilt crown embossed on the outside, 'that'll be for me; somebody at the Prime Minister's Office in Westminster Palace needs a package delivered back to Dublin, no doubt, and they think that I – the Keeper of the Irish Crown Jewels, no less – am their designated delivery boy.'

'Begging your pardon, Mr Stoker,' said the waiter, 'but it's addressed to Mr *Bram* Stoker, the younger Mr Stoker.'

Molly and Bram exchanged puzzled glances.

'And I'm afraid it's not from Westminster Palace,' continued the waiter, 'it's from *Buckingham* Palace.'

Thornley, about to put a mouthful of sausage into his open gob, dropped his silver fork with a clatter.

Bram reached up and snatched the letter from the quivering waiter's velvet cushion. It had an elaborate crown embossed on it, underneath which were the letters V and R. Bram opened the letter and read it out.

Buckingham Palace

Sunday, the 26th of July 1859

Dear Miss Malone and Master Stoker,

We were very grateful to hear about your daring rescue of my favourite author, Mr Charles Dickens.

'When she says *we*, Mol,' explained Bram, his voice shaking slightly, 'she means the Royal *we* – Queen Victoria always refers to herself as *we*.'

'The Royal Wee!' giggled Molly.

'That's *we,* not *wee!*' grinned Bram. He continued reading.

Please accept our heartiest congratulations and thanks for engaging in this doubtless very dangerous endeavour, and for delivering the Kingdom's most renowned author back to us.

Mr Dickens most assuredly puts the *Great* in Great Britain and we, for one, would not know what to do without his books.

'It's signed,' said Bram in a shaky voice, '*Victoria Regina*.'

'Old Queen Vic herself!' said Molly. 'She must love readin' his books while she's sittin' down, havin' the Royal *wee!*'

Suddenly there was a kerfuffle from the other end of the breakfast room, and the sound of scraping chairs as people who were eating their breakfast, put down their cutlery and stood up. Cries of 'It's him!' and 'Bravo, sir!' sounded, and some people clapped their hands as a bearded figure, dressed in a blue coat and with his loving son by his side, made his way towards the Stokers' breakfast table.

'Charles Dickens!' exclaimed an astonished Thornley, standing up and making an awkward half bow – Bram wasn't the only Stoker who adored Dickens' books!

'Miss Malone,' said the great author, with a twinkle in his eye, 'Master Bram Stoker, my boy Harry here has told me – in exquisite detail I might add – all about the trouble you took to rescue me from the clutches of the misguided Lady H. I wish to offer you both this humble gift as a token of my undying gratitude.' He placed a box on the table. Thornley, his eyes on the great man, opened the box. Inside was a full collection of every single one of Dickens' books, all leather bound and richly decorated with expensive gold filigree. 'They're all signed too!' said an awestruck Thornley, opening up a copy of *David Copperfield*.

Harry launched himself at Molly and hugged her tight.

'You have a lovely family here, Mr and Mrs Stoker,' said Dickens, putting his arm on Bram's shoulder. 'Family is the most important thing. Perhaps with all my work, I may have forgotten that.'

'Oh, Mr Dickens,' said Mama Stoker, 'we treasure all of our family.' She pulled Molly to her and hugged her. '*All* of them.'

'Well, young man,' Dickens said to Bram, 'I'd better be off – I have to get back to writing the next chapter of *A Tale of Two Cities*, and Harry has promised to show me some new magic tricks.'

He leaned in close to Bram's ear, 'By the way,' he said, 'I have read all of your letters, every single one, and I know all about your wish to one day become a writer. All I can say on that matter is, keep reading, young Bram Stoker, and keep writing, writing, writing. And most of all, keep on having adventures that inspire you!' He tapped a long finger thoughtfully against his beard. 'Do you know,' he said, 'that Lady H was a queer customer, a tragic woman spending years of her life never quite being able to get over a disappointment in her past – I may use her as a character in a book one day myself! Perhaps the H could stand for … *Hoggisham*?'

Harry tugged his father's sleeve. 'Or *Havisham*, Father!' he said.

'Havisham, it is!' cried Dickens, ruffling his son's hair. 'Much better! Less piggy-sounding! Clever boy!' He looked back at Bram. 'And speaking of books, I should very much love to one day read something that *you* have written – a book that I can really get my teeth into!'

'Oh,' said Harry, 'one last thing before we go.' With a theatrical flourish, he produced his black and white magic wand from beneath his black magician's cape and tapped the brim of the top hat he had been holding. Instantly, a colourful bunch of fresh flowers popped out from the upturned crown of the hat. Beaming a huge smile, Harry plucked the flowers from his topper and presented them to a very surprised Molly, chirping a high-pitched, 'Ta-DAAA!'

With that, Dickens and his son Harry, A.K.A. The Astounding Harry Dee, waved a cheery goodbye to the astonished Stoker family and walked out of the breakfast room to more cheers and claps on the back from the other diners.

Bram sat back into his comfortable dining chair and looked at his best friend Molly Malone. 'Write something he can get his teeth into?' he said. 'How did Charles Dickens know that I am trying to write about vampires?'

'I don't know, Quality,' said Molly with a grin, 'all I know is that it's almost time to go back to Dublin.'

'And as much as I liked London,' she said, sniffing at her bunch of flowers, 'there's absolutely, positively no place like home.'

* * *

After three or four months of serving at Her Majesty's (Queen Victoria's, not Molly's dog's) pleasure in Brixton Prison, Lady H decided that prison life suited her most admirably; there was a strict no-talking rule, so she was bothered by none of the other inmates, all of whom she found to be tiresome and giddy; she was allowed to wear her customary black clothes (in fact, the prison guards *insisted* that all the prisoners wore black at all times); no pets were allowed (she didn't miss Estella one little bit); and, best of all, Brixton Prison, although sombre, silent and chilly, boasted an extensive library.

Lady H had not been surprised at all to learn that Brixton Prison having a library was due in no small part to the venerable Mr Charles Dickens himself; it was a well-known fact that Dickens had campaigned vigorously for books to be provided to the poor, the destitute *and* to the incarcerated, with the hope that the act of reading might improve their outlook, their literacy and prospects of gainful employment, and, in the case of prison inmates, their chances of successful rehabilitation and return into society.

For this, Lady H silently thanked Charles Dickens most profusely. The one thing that had concerned her when the judge had banged his gavel and sent her to Brixton was that there would be no books to read when she got there. Instead, she found a quiet place where she was mostly left to her own devices: a home with free bed and board, and more books than she had ever imagined. As well as that, she found her five-year sentence had provided her with an enormous amount of time on her hands to read, read, read! She could almost find it in her heart to forgive Mr Dickens for what he had done to poor Little Nell in *The Old Curiosity Shop. Almost* …

Alone in the silent prison library, she ran her black lace-covered fingers along the row of books on the shelf, picking one at random. She studied the spine, *Moby-Dick* by Herman Melville, and sat down to read; it was all about a sea captain called Ahab who goes on the trail of a great white whale called Moby-Dick. After a couple of hours of solid reading, Lady H skipped ahead to the last page – she didn't like to be surprised and always read the ending of a book before she got too far into it.

As she read the final paragraphs of the book, her face beneath her black veil he began to turn a deeper and deeper shade of red, until it became almost purple in colour. She began to shake violently and her hands gripped the book so tightly that the paper pages began to rip. The prison librarian entered from a back room and put her finger to her lips. *SSSSSH-HHH*. Lady H forced herself to stop shaking and to re-read the final paragraphs. Poor Captain Ahab, the one-legged, rugged sea dog and by far her favourite character in the book, ends up being cruelly *killed* by the whale! *Correction*, she thought, *cruelly killed by THE AUTHOR!*

She slammed the book closed and, ignoring the signs that read *Silence in the Library,* stomped noisily over to the library desk, the KLIP-KLOP sound of her button-boot heels echoing off the room's high walls and barred windows. She angrily slapped the book down on the counter.

'WHERE,' demanded Lady H, with a furious snarl that made the Librarian cower, 'DOES THIS IDIOT AUTHOR HERMAN MELVILLE LIVE??'

Author's note on Dublin & London

Dublin:

Many of the Dublin locations in this book are as real as can be and can be visited today. Bram's home still stands at **19 Buckingham Street**; there is even a plaque to announce that he lived there, as well as a painting of his most famous character, *Dracula*, on the wall.

Kingstown, where Molly and Bram board the Steam Packet for Holyhead, is now known as **Dún Laoghaire** – ferries still set sail from there to Wales on a regular basis. Fairs take place at **Smithfield Market** to this day, but don't worry, they are seldom troubled nowadays by out-of-control runaway primates!

The dark narrow alleyway between Dame Street and Dame Lane is now called **Dame Court** and looks like it might *still* be top of Billy the Pan's list for a spot of *Blind-Man's-Buff*.

LONDON:

The imposing **Great Northern Hotel**, situated between St Pancras and King's Cross railway stations, is open for business today; the monumental **British Museum** is a short walk away at leafy Russell Square.

The **Houses of Parliament** at **Westminster Palace** and the adjoining **St Stephen's Clock Tower** with its **Big Ben** bell are popular tourist destinations to this day.

Almost unbelievably, **Ye Olde Cheshire Cheese** in Fleet Street is a *real* London tavern; visitors can sit at the table where Charles Dickens used to write. Above the bar is a stuffed parrot called Polly, who scandalised London in the 1920s with her fruity language – maybe she was a great granddaughter of the book's own foul-mouthed fowl, Myrtle?

Dickens' former London home at **48 Doughty Street** now houses the Charles Dickens Museum, which is well worth a visit – Dickens' speaking lectern (as depicted by Shane Cluskey on the cover of this book!) and the desk on which he wrote *Oliver Twist* can both be seen there.

The **Fishmongers' Hall**, home to the Worshipful Company of Fishmongers, is a real place (or 'a *real plaice*,' as the Company's butler might say) – it stands on the banks of the River Thames, beside **London Bridge**.

Lastly, you will be delighted to learn that **Jacob's Island** and the **River Neckinger** have been cleaned up quite a bit since the 1850s and can be found between the more modern Tower Bridge and a sandy stretch of the Thames shore called Bermondsey Beach.

Why not visit some of these places the next time you're in Dublin or London? They might even inspire you, just like Bram, to become a writer!

The Real Bram & Molly

Bram Stoker

The *real* Bram Stoker was born and raised in Marino Crescent in Clontarf. After school he attended Trinity College in Dublin, where was a star athlete. He always had a great love of writing and theatre, and after college he first became a newspaper theatre critic, and, after that, a theatre manager in London ... and then he decided to combined these two loves to write books such as *Dracula*, *The Lady in the Shroud*, and *The Lair of the White Worm*. His wife's name was Florence!

Molly Malone

Molly is *definitely* a fictional character, best known from the famous Dublin song where she roams the city streets selling cockles and mussels, '*alive alive-oh!*' She's a fishmonger in my book too, as well as a born leader, an accomplished pickpocket and 'the best sneak thief in Dublin'. But, to Bram, Molly is much more than that – she's a true and faithful friend.

The Song

Molly Malone

(Traditional)

In Dublin's fair city

Where the girls are so pretty

I first set my eyes on sweet Molly Malone

As she wheeled her wheelbarrow

Through streets broad and narrow

Crying, 'Cockles and mussels, alive, alive, oh!'

She was a fishmonger

And sure 'twas no wonder

For so were her father and mother before

And they both wheeled their barrows

Through streets broad and narrow

Crying, 'Cockles and mussels, alive, alive, oh!'

She died of a fever

And no one could save her

And that was the end of sweet Molly Malone

But her ghost wheels her barrow

Through streets broad and narrow

Crying, 'Cockles and mussels, alive, alive, oh!'

Alive, alive, oh

Alive, alive, oh

Crying 'Cockles and mussels, alive, alive, oh!'

Acknowledgements

Thanks to the inestimable Helen Carr, my amazing editor and good pal; to Ivan, Kunak, Ruth, Chloe, Brenda, Bex and all at the O'Brien Press; to Emma Byrne, designer extraordinaire; to Sarah Webb for her relentless upbeat book-y positivity; to Trish Hennessey and all the crew at the award-winning Halfway Up The Stairs Children's Bookshop in Greystones for all the support; to our Laureate na nÓg, Patricia Forde, a brilliant author and a fabulous bus companion – *go raibh maith agat*, Trish; to Shane Hegarty, Gary Northfield and Louie Stowell for the friendship and kind words (and extra thanks to Gary for his suggestion of having Mr Grimble and Mr Bleat use slightly wonky climbing gang, sorry, rhyming slang, throughout); to the ferociously talented Shane Cluskey for his amazing illustrations that bring the bould Molly'n'Bram to life; to Lily Pickle Joni Nolan for all the walks; and, lastly, to my long-suffering family who are always the first to hear my ideas and, strangely enough, are always the last to read them.

TURN THE PAGE TO DISCOVER MORE OF

MOLLY MALONE & BRAM STOKER'S ADVENTURES

Molly Malone & Bram Stoker in The Sackville Street Caper
by Alan Nolan
Cover illustration by Shane Cluskey

Eleven-year-old Bram Stoker, future author of *Dracula*, escapes school and runs away to 1850s Dublin City seeking adventure. There he meets Molly Malone, accomplished sneak thief and part time fishmonger. Together they must thwart the evil Count Vladimir who plans to steal the Irish Crown Jewels from Dublin Castle.

Molly Malone & Bram Stoker in Double Trouble at the Dead Zoo
by Alan Nolan
Cover illustration by Shane Cluskey

Molly and Bram's new friend Sanjit has come from India to stay with his professor uncle - but now his uncle has been KIDNAPPED! Can Bram and Molly, with the help of the Sackville Street Spooks, find out where the professor has gone? Can they follow the clues in an ancient treasure map and defeat the curse of the Dead Zoo?

Growing up with

tots to teens and in between

Why CHILDREN love O'Brien:

Over 350 books for all ages, including
picture books, humour, fiction, true stories,
nature and more

Why TEACHERS love O'Brien:

Hundreds of activities and teaching guides,
created by teachers for teachers,
all FREE to download from obrien.ie

Visit, explore, buy
obrien.ie